A PROTECTORS FAMILY CHRISTMAS

The Protectors #5.5

SLOANE KENNEDY

Contents

Copyright	v
A Protectors Family Christmas	vii
Trademark Acknowledgements	ix
Acknowledgments	xi
family	xiii
Chapter 1	1
Chapter 2	13
Chapter 3	20
Chapter 4	26
Chapter 5	30
Chapter 6	37
Chapter 7	43
Chapter 8	56
Chapter 9	65
Chapter 10	72
Chapter 11	78
Chapter 12	84
Chapter 13	90
Chapter 14	101
Chapter 15	111
Chapter 16	121
Chapter 17	124
Epilogue	130
Bonus Scene	136
Also by Sloane Kennedy	143

A Protectors Family Christmas is a work of fiction. Names, characters, businesses, places, events and incidents are either the products of the author's imagination or used in a fictitious manner. Any resemblance to actual persons, living or dead, or actual events is purely coincidental.

Copyright © 2016 by Sloane Kennedy

Published in the United States by Sloane Kennedy
All rights reserved. This book or any portion thereof may not be reproduced or used in any manner whatsoever without the express written permission of the publisher except for the use of brief quotations in a book review.

Copyright © Cover Design: Cate Ashwood Designs, 2019

ISBN:
9781539971702

A Protectors Family Christmas

Sloane Kennedy

Trademark Acknowledgements

The author acknowledges the trademarked status and trademark owners of the following trademarks mentioned in this work of fiction:

Star Wars/Darth Vader
Spiderman
Legos
X-men/Magneto

Acknowledgments

A big thank you to all my readers for continuing to inspire me with this series. The fact that you love my men as much as I do makes it even more of a pleasure to delve into their lives and share their stories with you.

Thank you to my regular beta readers who make sure I don't miss things when it comes to my guys' tales!

To my soul sisters, you make being in this insane business a whole lot more easy…and fun!

Hope everyone has an amazing, safe and joyous holiday season!

family

noun fam·i·ly, \\'fam-le\\

Family is who you say your family is
--Anonymous

Chapter 1

RONAN

"I'M TELLING YOU, IT NEEDS TO GO DOWN HERE," WAS THE FIRST thing I heard a heavy voice say as I walked down the narrow hallway leading to what I knew was the kitchen near the back of the house. Baby, the Rottweiler, had met me at the door, but hadn't barked when I'd knocked and when I'd finally opened it after there was no answer, the big dog had wiggled his butt in excitement and then had begun sniffing my pockets, presumably for the hot dogs he so loved and that visitors often made a habit of sneaking him.

"No, they'll take him down for sure if it happens here...he's got no advantage."

The first voice had been Memphis's, the second Hawke's. I had no clue what they were arguing about, but it was clearly some kind of mission, which was odd considering Hawke had left the team months earlier and even now was in the process of going legit by signing on with Dominic Barretti's security firm.

"This is fucking insane," I heard Mav grumble and I didn't miss the edge of tension in his voice. He was the reason I'd stopped by on the way home from the hospital. His text had been brief and vague.

My place as soon as you can.

I'd called Mav just to make sure it wasn't some kind of emergency, but his clipped tone when he'd told me it wasn't and just to get there as soon as I could had been enough for me to beg off my last meeting of the day with the Chief of Trauma Surgery at Seattle Med, the hospital I was going to be working at, once I completed the recertification process. I wasn't worried that my new boss would be pissed about the whole thing because he'd made it more than clear that he was excited to have me joining the staff, and he hadn't bothered to hide the fact that it was how I'd saved young Brennan Devereaux's life that had played a big role in fast tracking the entire process for me.

I didn't announce my presence as I entered the kitchen and surprisingly, not one of the three men who I considered some of the most lethal killers I'd ever met, noticed me. Memphis and Hawke were bent over a huge piece of paper spread out on the kitchen table and Mav was pacing back and forth in front of the patio doors that led out onto a small porch. The rental house that Mav and Eli had selected wasn't very big, but I could tell they'd been working to make it their own. I could still smell the fresh paint from the newly finished walls and I could see that many of the out of date appliances that had come with the place had been replaced with gleaming black ones that contrasted nicely with the white cabinets and dark gray countertop.

"I think this whole thing is going to hinge on misdirection," another voice said and I realized it was Mace's voice coming over the speaker of a cell phone sitting on the kitchen table.

"And we need to make sure he isn't outnumbered...anything more than three to one and he's fucked," Memphis pointed out.

Hawke shook his head. "Nope, I'd say two to one...these guys are good."

"Everything okay in here?" I asked as I studied the stiffness in Mav's normally relaxed frame. Memphis and Hawke barely spared me a glance as they waved me over.

"Ronan, good...come check this out and tell us what you think. We're thinking about a blitz approach," Hawke said calmly as his finger roamed over the paper in front of him.

"*This* is how they help," Mav snapped as he whirled around and motioned to the two men.

I'd never seen Mav so agitated and a sliver of worry went through me. "What's going on? Is Eli okay?" I automatically asked because that was the only thing I could think of that would have the normally cool-as-stone Mav so upset.

"It was supposed to be simple. In and out," he muttered before crossing his arms, almost like he was trying to soothe himself. "Then these morons show up…"

I glanced at Memphis and Hawke who had finally turned around to look at me. "He was going to just walk in there blind, Ronan," Hawke said, a wan smile gracing his lips. I didn't miss the hint of amusement in his eyes and I instantly relaxed. I still didn't have a clue what was going on, but it clearly wasn't a life or death situation.

"What's the mission?" I finally said as I shrugged my coat off. It was late November in Seattle which meant on and off cold rain and drizzle on most days.

It was Hawke who answered by reaching behind him for something on the table. I couldn't help but smile when I saw the small black velvet box, the top flipped open to reveal a shiny white gold ring with a black inlay. I had no doubt who it was for, but one glance at Mav who was still fidgeting as he stared at the ring and I forced the smile away.

"May I?" I asked Mav as Hawke handed me the box.

Mav's dark green eyes flipped up to meet mine and he finally nodded jerkily. I carefully removed the ring from its velvet bed and held it up so I could get a better look. The piece of jewelry was stunning and I could tell that Mav had dropped a pretty penny for it. Some writing on the inside of the ring caught my eye.

A lifetime of firsts.

Emotion welled up in my chest because I knew exactly what the words meant…Eli had given Mav so many firsts…love, family, a home.

"It's beautiful," I murmured and then returned my gaze to Mav. "He'll love it," I reassured him.

Mav relaxed marginally and nodded. I didn't need any more than that so I gently put the ring back and then handed the box to him. "So what is all this?" I asked as I motioned to Memphis and Hawke.

"He asked us to help him come up with a plan to pop the question."

I glanced at Mav and said, "Mav, you know he'll say yes…he doesn't need some elaborate plan."

"Uh, Ronan," I heard Mace say from the phone. "The question's not for Eli."

Memphis grabbed the phone and held it, presumably so Mace wouldn't miss any of the conversation. "He needs to ask a certain someone for permission," Memphis said quietly, though I didn't miss the smirk that stole across his features. All three men were having entirely too much fun at Mav's expense.

"Dom," I said in understanding. Dominic Barretti may not have been Eli's biological father, but he loved the young man as fiercely as he loved his own children. I speared Memphis with my gaze and said, "Just remember, when the day comes, you're going to need to talk to him about his son *and* his nephew."

The reminder caused Memphis to pale and I heard Hawke chuckle. When my eyes slipped to him, he held his hands up and said, "Hey, I got permission from Tate's mom."

"Tate's mom adores you," I responded. "You got off easy."

"True," Hawke agreed and he quieted.

"Mace," I said firmly.

"Yeah, I'm with you," Mace answered through the phone, his voice suddenly less jovial and I had no doubt he was thinking about the fact that he also had several people to go through when he decided to pop the question to his partners. "Sorry, Mav, we really do want to help."

"I'm not asking permission," Mav grumbled as he fingered the jewelry box. "I'm just letting Dom know as a courtesy. Like I did with Eli's mom."

"Mariana knows?" I asked.

Mav nodded. "She was…emotional."

I chuckled because I had no doubt there had been lots of waterworks and Mav was definitely not fond of waterworks.

"Mav," I said as I walked up to him and patted him on the shoulder. "Dom's going to be fine with it."

Another nod, but Mav's eyes dropped to the box in his hand. "He's going to be a doctor, Ronan," Mav said softly. I knew then what Mav was struggling with and I hated that even after the four months he and Eli had been together, his insecurities that he wasn't one hundred percent good enough for Eli or the young man's big, powerful, successful family still gnawed at him. And I suspected he'd kept those feelings well hidden from his soon-to-be fiancé.

I glanced at Hawke and Memphis who'd gone completely silent and saw the compassion lingering in their eyes. They clearly hadn't understood the reason behind Mav's agitation. I turned my focus back on Mav and asked, "Has he ever given you a reason to doubt him or what he feels for you?"

Mav's head snapped up. "No! Of course not!"

"Then the rest is just noise, right? Even if by some wild stretch of the imagination Dom says you aren't good enough for Eli, do you think it will change Eli's answer?"

Mav shook his head. "No," he finally admitted.

"Call it a courtesy or call it permission – it doesn't change the end result. Eli is yours. He's always been yours and he always will be. His job won't change that, his family won't change that, your fears won't change that."

Mav didn't respond, but he did take a deep breath and I saw some of the tension ease out of him.

"Now, I don't think you'll need it, but if it makes you feel better, I've got the solution to your problem with all this," I said as I waved my hand at the paper on the table which actually looked like a drawing of the interior of Dom and Logan Barretti's island house. "Two words." I held up my hand to count off the words. "Pinch," I said firmly as I lifted one finger. "Hitter," I added as I raised another finger.

Mav's eyes settled on my hand for a moment and then he smiled.

"Matty," was all he said.

I glanced over my shoulder at Hawke and Memphis and said, "And that's how it's done."

I FELT MY BODY COME ALIVE WITH EXCITEMENT AS I PULLED PAST THE iron gate and began the long drive up the driveway. It was a sensation I knew I would never lose, not as long as I knew Seth was waiting for me to come home. It had been just eight months since I'd stolen back into his life and they'd been the best eight months of my entire fucking life. Yeah, there'd been those few weeks early on where I'd nearly driven him away with my cruelty and lies, but Seth had been the stronger one and he'd kept coming back to me no matter how many times I'd pushed him away. And now he was mine in every sense of the word.

My thoughts drifted back to my own proposal, though it could barely be called that since there'd been no planning or fanfare. Hell, I hadn't even had a ring. Nope, it hadn't been conventional at all – just me buried deep inside of Seth's beautiful body, his luminous eyes staring at mine as he'd clung to me, his lips parted as he'd whispered my name. I'd watched a tear slip down his smooth cheek as I'd rolled my hips against his and I'd known.

Because how could I not want everything with the young man who still felt the emotion so keenly every time we came together?

I'd slowed my movements only long enough to lean down and kiss the tear before pulling back enough so I could see his eyes as I'd whispered, "Marry me," to him. He'd held my gaze for the longest time, but there hadn't been any shock or surprise in his eyes. No, he'd known it was coming at some point. His faith in me was that unfailing. There'd been no tears or gasps or exclamations…his eyes had simply held mine as he'd slowly nodded and the smallest of smiles had graced his lips. And then his hand had come up to cup my face as our bodies had taken over our lovemaking. It was something he knew I liked…him touching me with every part of himself.

It was something I still couldn't believe I'd ever thought I could go without.

We'd gotten married just a week later, both because we hadn't wanted to wait even a moment longer than we had to, and because we'd wanted Matty and his fathers to be able to attend. Our relationship with Hawke and Tate had strengthened a thousand times over in the months we'd continued to help them support Matty during his treatments for leukemia, but it was our connection to the little boy that had changed a lot of things for Seth and me. Even though Hawke had only asked us to watch out for Matty early on when Hawke and Tate were in Texas to deal with Tate's father and brother, the bond we'd formed with the child had done something to us both that I still couldn't explain and we hadn't wanted, or even been able, to give up our daily visits with him even after Hawke and Tate had returned. In so many ways he'd become our son in that first week that we'd spent with him and it had been the most natural thing for us to continue to be a part of his life and he ours in the weeks and months that had followed.

Since I had already started the process of handing the reins of my group over to Memphis and Mav, it had been easy for me to commit to playing a full-time role in supporting Matty. But Seth had been different. He'd just been in the process of fully taking on all the responsibilities that came with running a successful shipping company when Hawke had asked us to help with Matty for that week. There'd been no issue with Seth taking the time off from work…he hadn't even hesitated for a second. But when Hawke and Tate had returned and settled into their new roles of co-parenting the little boy, along with Matty's grandfather, Magnus, something in Seth had shifted. He'd been free to go back to work on whatever schedule he'd wanted, but I'd sensed the reluctance in him to do so. When I'd finally realized how much he'd been struggling with splitting his time between the company he felt an obligation to and the little boy he'd fallen completely in love with, I'd told him it was his right to choose one over the other. I'd known it wouldn't be an easy choice for him since the company was all he had left of his father, but he'd chosen Matty and had taken an extended leave of absence from work, though he'd assured me – and likely himself – that it was just until Matty was out of the hospital. But Matty had finally been released from the hospital this past week and Seth still seemed to be struggling with the idea of going back to work.

I slowed my car as I saw Bullet tear out of the house and run down the driveway towards me. It was an odd little ritual we'd picked up early on and I couldn't help but laugh at the dog's antics as he jumped next to the driver's side window, his barks growing louder and louder until I finally stopped the car and opened my door. I groaned when one of the dog's paws hit me in the nuts as he climbed over my body to sit in the passenger seat. "Every time," I muttered to Bullet as I pulled the door closed. I could see Seth hovering on the steps leading up to the house as I pulled into the circular part of the driveway, and I immediately noticed his agitation. I barely remembered to put the car in park before getting out. I kept my eyes on Seth as I waited for Bullet to get out. I hadn't seen my husband looking so tense in a long time. He didn't look like he was about to have a panic attack though; fortunately, those had diminished early on in our relationship as he'd become more accustomed to being around larger groups of people.

"Baby," I said softly to Seth when I reached him and took his hands in mine. His big eyes settled on me and then he wrapped his arms around my neck. Since he was higher up on the stairs than me, it was easy for him to settle his face against mine and I softly whispered into his ear, "Did something happen?"

Seth shook his head and just held on to me. I ran my hands up and down his back and felt him relax somewhat. He finally pulled back and kissed me softly. "I just really wanted to see you," was all he said, and then he settled his mouth on mine. I couldn't stifle the moan that bubbled up from my throat as his tongue slipped into my mouth and mated with mine. When we were finally forced to come up for air, I pulled him against me again and just held him.

"Do you want to go for a walk?" I asked, since I knew there was definitely something he needed to get off his chest.

Seth nodded against my neck and then reached for my hand. I followed him through the house and into the backyard. Neither of us spoke as we made our way down to the beach. Despite the cool, misty weather, Bullet darted into the water and began chasing the waves as they lapped up onto the shore. I held on to Seth's hand as we walked and didn't push him to tell me what was going on. I hadn't ever actually seen him this nervous before, at least not since we'd gotten past our rocky beginning, and that had me on edge.

"I had lunch with Connor and Zane today," Seth finally began after several long minutes of tense silence. I knew he'd grown close to both men since their son had become Matty's best friend in the past couple of months, but I didn't comment since I also knew that wasn't the crux of what had him so troubled.

"I drove because Connor doesn't drive and Zane's car was in the shop. Connor and I picked Zane up at his office. It was some kind of in-service day at Connor's school so he didn't have to work."

I nodded in understanding, suspecting Seth was somewhat rambling because he was building up to whatever was bothering him.

"During lunch, Zane got a call from the hospital. Some kids he's representing got hurt and were in the ER."

I didn't interrupt Seth because I was well aware that Zane Devereaux was an attorney who specialized in family law and was an advocate for kids in the judicial system. I admired the man for the work he did because I suspected he saw the worst of the worst when it came to the most innocent of victims.

"I drove him there and Connor and I went in with him."

When Seth didn't speak and refused to look at me, I asked, "Did you see the kids he was talking about?"

Seth nodded and I pulled him to a stop, hating that he was still refusing to look at me.

"Were they okay?"

He finally lifted his head and said, "The little girl broke her arm. I guess some of the other kids in the group home were hassling her and her brother and she fell off a bunk bed when one of the older boys tried to grab her."

"And her brother?" I asked.

"Not hurt...but he wouldn't leave her side, Ronan. They just... they just kept holding on to each other like..."

Seth's voice dropped off and I saw tears fill his eyes. "They don't even have real names."

I put my hand on his neck and began rubbing his cool, damp skin in the hopes of comforting him. "What do you mean?"

"Zane says neither of them have talked since they were brought in almost a week ago so no one knows their names. I guess the cops found them in an abandoned building of some kind downtown. It was just the two of them."

"How old are they?"

"They think the girl is eight or nine and the boy is around three. The girl...she's deaf and she won't respond to any kind of sign language. Zane says it will make it harder to find a foster family for her, but the boy is young enough..."

Seth's voice dropped off and I finally understood what he was struggling with. And truth be told, I didn't have a fucking clue how to feel about it. We'd managed to make our way back to where we'd started our walk and I tugged Seth down to sit on the weathered log that had long ago washed up on the shore and that was often the place we just sat and talked and held on to one another when we were admiring the view of the water and mountains beyond. I ignored the fact that the dampness of the log was seeping through my pants and pulled Seth against my side so that he wouldn't get too chilled.

"They're going to have to split them up," I murmured as I gave voice to what was bothering Seth.

"I know it's not fair to ask this, Ronan," Seth finally said as he sat up so he could look at me. "We've...we've never talked about the future and..."

"Kids," I finished for him.

Seth nodded and dropped his eyes. "I didn't even know it was something I wanted until Matty."

I tipped his face up and said, "Me neither," I murmured as I let my thumb skirt over his jawline. "But I do," I admitted.

A shimmer of relief spread across his features, but didn't last long. "They...they tried to take the little boy away from his sister when they had to cast her arm and he lost it...they both did," Seth murmured and then he wiped at his face, presumably to dash away the tears that were threatening to fall. "Even after they sedated her, he wouldn't let her go...I sat down near him and started showing him pictures of Bullet. And then I showed him how to work the camera and use that app that lets you add funny effects to the pictures you take..."

I nodded in understanding, hating the desperation in his voice. I knew exactly where he was heading, but I was conflicted about how I felt about it. What he was asking would literally change our entire lives.

"Can I see the pictures?" I asked when Seth's voice dropped off again.

He dug out his phone and unlocked it and then handed it to me. There were dozens of pictures of little body parts like a foot and a hand. There were some of Seth too and different people in the hospital room. Some were in weird colors and some had funny shapes added to them like an extra pair of lips or eyes. But my eyes focused on the last picture which the boy had managed to snap of himself. My first thought was that he was way too thin. His tear-stained face looked gaunt and his expression hollow as he stared at the camera. But there was a spark of something else there too...a shadow of curiosity that I instantly wanted to see more of. But what I really wanted to see was that slightly downturned mouth pull up into a smile. Except there were no pictures like that.

Not one.

"If we do this, it won't be easy," I said as I handed Seth his phone.

Seth nodded. "I...I can't explain it, Ronan, but I just...walking out of there and leaving them behind - it hurt in a way I can't explain," Seth murmured as his hand went to his chest and began rubbing back and forth. I had no doubt he was thinking about the night he'd lost his parents and what had remained of his idyllic childhood. "I know it will change everything, but I don't want it to change what we have..."

I knew what he was talking about and I realized he wasn't taking this whole thing lightly. Yes, he was clearly emotionally invested, but he'd also been thinking about more than just the immediate need to protect the kids. I clasped my hand around the back of his neck as I shifted my body so I was straddling the log. I drew him forward until our lips met, but I kept the kiss brief. "Nothing will ever change what we have. We may be tested by whatever the future brings, but *we* won't be changed by it, do you hear me? We're in this together until the end."

Seth turned his head to kiss my palm and then he practically crawled into my lap. He put his forehead against mine and whispered, "I wake up every morning thanking God for bringing you back into my life."

"I wake up every morning thanking *you* for not letting me walk out of it again," I said softly and then I kissed him. And I kept kissing him until the damp chill of the evening air began to settle around us. I once again took his hand in mine as we began walking back towards the house, Bullet now walking sedately next to us. And I couldn't help but think how different things would look if there were five of us instead of three. A quick glance at Seth showed he was thinking the same thing and I knew then that I'd do my best to make things right by those kids.

I'd do it for them and for Seth…and for me.

Chapter 2

HAWKE

THE SECOND I OPENED THE DOOR, A BUNDLE OF DENIM WAS THRUST at me and I looked down to see young Leo Devereaux standing on the threshold wearing only a thin long-sleeved shirt, a pair of white underwear with Darth Vader on them and bright red sneakers. His jacket was lying on the walkway leading up to the house. I looked up at the house across the street and saw Zane Devereaux shaking his head from where he stood in his own doorway.

"Hey, Leo," I said with a chuckle as I stepped aside. "He's in his room."

"Thanks," the boy said brightly and then he disappeared into the house as I went out to grab his jacket. I glanced over my shoulder just in time to see his shirt hit the floor as he rounded the corner to go down the hallway to Matty's room. I laughed and gave Zane a wave as I snagged the jacket and I watched the other man disappear into his house. I spared a quick glance at Dante Thorne who was sitting in a sedate blue sedan at the end of the block. His eyes met mine, but we didn't acknowledge each other since the goal was for him to remain as invisible as possible. Ronan and I had decided we'd have Dante shadow Matty until after the holidays just to make one hundred percent sure that Tate's and my past was no longer a threat to us or our son. While Zane and his husband knew about the reason for Dante's presence, none of the other neighbors did and I wanted to keep it that way.

Tate and I had lucked out when we'd discovered that the house across the street from Matty's new best friend's house was up for sale and we'd immediately put an offer in on it. And the slight bidding war with another set of buyers that had followed hadn't deterred us in the least. It wasn't that the house was even our dream house or anything, at least not in the typical sense. No, it was what the house represented that had us paying considerably more than it was worth. It was moments like these where Matty's best friend could come over to play that had made it worth every extra penny we'd spent. Knowing our son could ride his bike with his friends in the quiet cul-de-sac or that he could wait at the bus stop with the boy he never stopped talking about…those had been the reasons we'd snatched up the house.

We'd been in the house less than a week when Matty had finally gotten the all clear three days ago to leave the hospital for what we hoped would be the last time. It had been a roller coaster of emotions since then, as we'd started the process of adjusting to a normal life again after spending so many weeks in the hospital at Matty's bedside. There was, of course, the unbelievable joy that we finally got to walk our son out of those hospital doors for what would hopefully be the last time, but there was also the intense uncertainty as we waited to learn if our son was officially in remission. And even just adjusting to the most normal of tasks like going to the grocery store or trying to decide what to make for dinner was a challenge. From the moment Tate and I had met, nothing about our lives had been normal and trying to be that now was daunting to say the least.

I went back into the house and grabbed Leo's shirt and then went to Matty's room to make sure the boys were getting on okay. I found them sitting in front of Matty's closet surrounded by superhero action figurines and Storm, Matty's puppy who now weighed more than he did, was lying on his bed chewing on one of her dog toys. They were deep in conversation about some kind of attack they were planning on the enemy and didn't notice me which was exactly the way I wanted it. My son was finally being the kid he deserved to be. I turned to go, not missing the fact that Leo was now wearing Matty's favorite Spiderman shirt. The pants were still a no-go though and I stifled a laugh as I thought of poor Zane and Connor trying to keep up with their tenacious son.

I walked down the hallway to Tate's and my bedroom and found my fiancé sitting on our bed, a notebook open in his lap and pages of notes scattered around him. We were still waiting for some of our furniture to be delivered so I knew the bed was the best place for Tate to spread things out. He glanced up at me and paused in whatever he was writing down and I felt my heart clench at the look in his eyes. No matter how stressed or worried he was about all the changes we faced, there was always this moment when he looked at me and all I saw was contentment. Like he was exactly where he was supposed to be. It was a feeling I knew all too well.

"Leo?" Tate asked with a chuckle as he glanced at the clothes in my hand.

I nodded and put the clothes on the end of the bed. "I think I found his Kryptonite, though," I said as I sat down on the bed and began moving papers out of the way so I could get closer to my man.

"Oh yeah? What?"

"Let's just say our son's taste in fashion is rubbing off on him."

Tate smiled and then reached next to him to grab a small spiral bound notebook. I saw him jot something down. I took the notebook from him before he could put it away again. It was a Christmas list and I could see Leo's name on it and a note about superhero clothing. There were a half a dozen names on the list besides mine and Matty's and when I turned to the next page, I saw more names. I flipped back to the first page.

"I don't know what to get you," Tate murmured as his hand came up to play with the back of my neck. A shiver ran down my spine and my cock automatically stiffened to full attention.

I fingered the gold band on Tate's left hand and whispered, "You've already given me exactly what I wanted." I leaned in and brushed my mouth over his. "Everything I've ever wanted." When Tate's tongue licked over mine, I pressed against him with the intention of getting him flat on his back, but the rustling papers beneath my leg reminded me we weren't really free to do more so I pulled back and said, "What is all this?"

"Wedding stuff," Tate said as he pointed to one section. "Bills," – he pointed to the middle section – "And Christmas." He put the notebook back down next to him and shook his head. "A Christmas wedding," he murmured. "What were we thinking?"

Despite our plan to keep the wedding simple, it was still proving to be anything but simple to actually plan it. Add in the stress of trying to set up a new house and prepare for our first Christmas together, and I had to wonder why we hadn't given the idea more thought. But I knew the answer. We'd wanted to end this year as the family we were meant to be. We'd wanted to celebrate all the many things we had to be thankful for and we'd wanted to do it during a time that had always been painful for each of us in the years before we'd found each other.

"The venue called and said they couldn't accommodate all the people anymore because the ballroom they had us set up in sustained water damage from a leaking pipe and the only room they have left is half the size. But the invitations have already gone out..." Tate glanced at the other stacks of papers and shook his head. "If I don't get started on the Christmas shopping, I won't get it all done in time and we've got all these appointments this week." Tate held up a piece of paper with several dates and times on them. I knew they were a mix of doctor appointments for Matty as well as things like getting the phone and cable set up in the house.

"We could postpone," I offered as I began looking through some of the paperwork.

Tate shook his head and looked at me. "I don't want to wait even a minute longer than I have to to marry you," he said softly.

I nodded because I felt the same way. I knew we could easily go down to the courthouse at any time and make things official, but I didn't want that. I wanted to be surrounded by our family and friends. I wanted the pomp and circumstance that went with committing myself forever to this one person. This person who'd changed me…saved me.

"Let me take care of this," I said as I nodded at the wedding papers. "We'll split these up," I added as I motioned to the list of appointments. "And I'll talk to Magnus about babysitting for a day or two and we'll get a jump on the Christmas shopping."

Tate looked at all the papers and then nodded. He dropped his head against my shoulder and I leaned back against the headboard, taking him with me. I would never tire of feeling his weight against my chest or the way his fingers would automatically slip under the collar of my shirt and seek out the tattoo on my skin…his tattoo. Or the brief caress he'd give the ring I still wore around my neck…the ring the first love of my life had given to me so many years ago.

After I'd proposed to Tate, I wasn't sure how he'd feel about me still wearing the wedding ring Revay had slipped on my finger so long ago. I'd tried taking the ring off after that, ignoring the bone-deep pain that had filtered through me as I'd put it in a small box and stashed it in one of the dresser drawers of the hotel we were living in at the time. But that night as I'd started making love to Tate, he'd asked me what had happened to it. When I'd told him I'd taken it off, he hadn't said a word – not one single word. He'd merely climbed out of bed, walked over to the dresser and searched first the top of it where we often left our keys and wallets and then finally the drawers until he'd found it. I'd been too overwhelmed to speak and when he'd crawled back into bed with it and carefully put the chain the ring was on back around my neck, I'd cried. He'd whispered that Revay would always belong with us and then he'd held me until I'd fallen asleep.

I hadn't even considered taking the ring off after that.

"I still can't believe all this is real," Tate murmured as I let my fingers trail up and down his spine.

"Me either," I admitted. "I keep thinking I'm going to wake up and I'll be back at the ranch listening to you drive away in your rental car."

Even the brief memory of nearly losing Tate forever had a chill racing through me.

"That was one of the worst days of my life," Tate said softly and I felt his fingertips press into my side as if preparing to stop me from escaping him.

I was prevented from saying anything else when I heard Matty call out, "Daddy, Papa!" and I heard footsteps coming down the hallway. Neither Tate nor I moved since Matty was used to seeing us embracing and sure enough, when he came to a stop in the doorway, he looked at Leo who stopped next to him and then said, "Told you."

Leo nodded. "My daddies kiss a lot too." Leo shook his head dramatically and I heard Tate chuckle.

"What's up guys?" I asked as I released Tate from my grip and we both straightened to an upright position on the bed. Matty walked across the room and climbed onto the bed. Leo followed behind and didn't hesitate to crawl up after Matty.

"Can we go get our Christmas tree now?" Matty asked, forcing an unnatural pout to his lip that made it hard for me to keep my expression neutral. I knew I would live for days like these where Matty behaved like every other little kid.

"We were going to go this weekend, buddy," Tate reminded him. Matty's face fell even further into a hang dog look and then he crawled between us until I was forced to move over to give him room. He snuggled up against Tate and gave him the worst sad eyes I'd ever seen.

"Please, Daddy?"

I would have smiled, but I was too busy shifting even more when Leo followed and pressed up against Matty to add his own hang dog look. And then Storm was hopping up and down next to the bed to get in on the action, but she wasn't quite big enough to actually jump on it. I gave in and reached down to grab her and pulled her up onto my lap. But she bypassed me and settled right on Tate's lap and stared at him with her big brown eyes.

Tate laughed and shook his head and then looked at me. "I've got nothing," he said ruefully.

"Yeah, you never had a chance." To the boys I said, "Okay, let's go. Matty go get your shoes and jacket. Leo, pants...and leave them on, okay?" I said as I motioned to Leo's clothes on the foot of the bed. "I'll call your dads and see if they want to go."

"Yay!" Matty shouted and then he carefully got off the bed. He was still weak as he recovered from his final chemo treatment, but other than slowing him down a bit, he was starting to act more and more like every other little kid. By the time the kids and dog were gone, Tate's papers were all over the bed and floor.

"Leave them," I said when he started to reach for them. "We'll get them later. Let's go take our son Christmas tree shopping."

Tate smiled and then leaned over to kiss me heatedly. His tongue stroked over mine and I felt his hand graze my cock through my pants. When he finally pulled back, I tried to follow, but he put his hand on my chest and whispered against my lips, "Consider that a preview of what's to come." His mouth brushed over mine in a feather-light kiss and then he was climbing off the bed.

"Tease," I muttered as I adjusted myself to try to somehow make more room in my pants.

Tate laughed and then came around to my side of the bed. "You love it," he said with a smile and then his face grew serious as he reached out to caress my cheek.

"Yeah I do," I responded quietly as I held his hand against my skin.

No other words needed to be said. We held each other's gazes for a moment before I took Tate's hand in mine and climbed off the bed. I managed to remember to grab Leo's pants and jacket since he'd managed to forget them and then I followed Tate out of the room and towards the sound of our son's laughter.

Chapter 3

MAV

"Yes," Eli whispered as his inner muscles tightened on my cock. "Right there."

A sigh escaped his lips as I slowly pulled my dick almost all the way out of him before sliding back in, making sure to nail his prostate just so as I did. He arched up as sensation flooded through him and I felt his fingers digging into my arms where he was holding onto me. His legs were wrapped around me, his heels digging into my ass as he tried to force me deeper inside of him.

But I was as deep as I could go.

I kissed him languidly as I held myself still inside of him, despite the way his body pulsed around my shaft. He was definitely close. Which wasn't a surprise considering I'd been fucking him for at least an hour without letting him come. Every time he'd come close, I'd pulled out of him and kissed and licked my way all over his body until his passion had cooled and then I'd slid back into him and fucked him slowly.

I could tell he both hated and loved my sensual torture.

But I wasn't going to rush anything with Eli now that I finally had him to myself for a little while. With the demands of his insanely busy schedule, there were days when I didn't even get to talk to him, much less make love to him.

"Mav, please," he begged as he slid his hands down my back.

"What, baby?" I asked, though I knew perfectly well what he wanted…needed.

"So close," he breathed against my mouth as he rolled his hips against mine. But there was only so much stimulation he could get from moving against me since I weighed so much more than him.

"Eli, open your eyes," I ordered and he instantly did. "I'm gonna let you come, baby, but then I'm gonna start all over again, okay?"

"Come with me," he urged.

I pulled out of him before shoving in hard and deep and he let out a loud moan. "No," I said as I did the move again. "Wanna see you come apart."

I didn't give him a chance to argue with me as I rolled my hips against his again. He cried out in pleasure and I felt my own balls tighten. Fuck, I might not even be able to keep my promise.

I reached behind me to grab Eli's hands and I pinned them both to the bed by the wrists. I held him down as I increased my thrusts and Eli bucked against me desperately as his orgasm began to take over. I could feel his cock leaking against my abdomen and I knew he was so far gone he wouldn't need any extra stimulation at all. Which was good because I didn't want to release him as I began ruthlessly fucking him. I hated to think it was part of my earlier insecurities resurfacing and I was trying to regain some semblance of control by the extra show of dominance, but clearly it wasn't bothering Eli in the least because he was frantically urging me on with his body and words.

"God, yes, harder Mav, please! Fuck, I love you so much!" Eli bit out as his eyes opened and held mine.

"Tell me you're mine!" I demanded as I suddenly came to a complete stop.

Eli let out a ragged whimper, but managed to get out, "Yours, Mav! Only yours!"

I slammed into him. "Again!"

"I'm yours, Mav. Always yours!"

I pounded into him again so hard that he would have slid up the bed if I hadn't been holding him down. He had absolutely no control, but I knew that, in reality, he was the one with all the power. But I also knew it wasn't something he would ever use against me.

It took just three more hard strokes to finish him and when he screamed in blissful agony, it was my name that he called out. His inner muscles clamped down on my dick and despite my promise that I was going to let him come and then start all over, I felt my own orgasm start to roll over me in a violent wave. I let out a harsh curse as I rammed into Eli, his muscles pressing down on my dick, causing my orgasm to climb even higher. I released his hands and wrapped my arms around his upper body, dragging him against my chest. His fingers bit into my shoulders as my body began to jerk against his and my release shot from my aching cock. Tears stung my eyes at how good it felt and as my hot cum bathed my own dick, I searched out Eli's mouth and kissed him as I rode out the uncontrollable pleasure of my orgasm. When the intense pleasure/pain finally eased, I dropped all my weight on my lover and tried to catch my breath. Eli's huffs in my ear told me he wasn't any better off than me. But when I tried to move off him even a little, he tightened his hold on me and I felt one of his hands close over my ass to urge me even deeper inside of him. The delicious aftershocks were still rippling through me so I tucked myself up into Eli's body until there was no place left to go and then I kissed him.

"Missed this," Eli murmured tiredly between soft kisses.

"Me too," I admitted.

Eli's hand brushed my hair back from my face and over my shoulder. "Mav, I know this has been hard-"

I cut him off with a kiss. "We're making it work, Eli. That's all that matters."

He nodded solemnly, but I knew it still bothered him. We'd both logically known that medical school would be a huge commitment and that our time together would become much more limited, but the reality of it was even worse. The sheer exhaustion Eli was dealing with from classes and studying was overwhelming and I was forced to watch helplessly as he tried to endure it. That wasn't to say he didn't enjoy his studies because he did. But trying to balance the demands of his education and our relationship wasn't easy on either of us and we knew it would only get worse as the years went on. But I wouldn't change any of it.

Not one thing.

The pride at knowing this smart, passionate, beautiful young man was all mine went beyond anything I could explain. But I hated that it also drove my most secret insecurities. In my heart, I knew Eli would always put me first, but my head was playing many of the games with me that it had when I'd been younger. And instead of trying to convince me that Eli would leave me, it was trying to tell me that I was holding him back. It was a voice that had grown louder and louder after I'd bought the engagement ring a few days ago.

It hadn't been a spur of the moment thing…I'd known from the first day that we'd moved in together that I wanted it to be permanent…that I wanted to bind Eli to me in any and every way that I could. Hell, I'd known that from almost the moment I'd met him. But when I'd gotten the ring home, I'd panicked as I'd thought about what Eli's family would think. Like I'd told Ronan and the guys, my plan hadn't necessarily been to ask Dom for permission to marry his son, but the more I thought about it, the more I realized that his approval was exactly what I was seeking. Which made no sense since the man hadn't ever given me the impression that he didn't think I was good enough for the kid he shared no blood with, but who he thought of as his just the same.

No one in the entire Barretti clan had made me feel that way either, but my brain was convinced that behind closed doors, it was a different story. I forced the disturbing thoughts away and focused on Eli's sated body. His lids were heavy so I carefully pulled free of him. His eyes fluttered back open and he wrapped his arms around my neck. I rolled us so that I was on my back and he was curled against my side, his head resting beneath my chin.

"I love you Mav," he whispered against me, his breath gently washing over my skin.

"I love you too," I said softly before dropping my mouth to kiss the top of his head. "Just sleep, Eli," I urged and I felt him snuggle into me. I knew he couldn't have been all that comfortable with the evidence of his release cooling all over his stomach and chest, but he couldn't fight his exhaustion and he was asleep within a couple of minutes anyway. I'd clean him up later, but for now I just needed to hang on to him.

The four months we'd been together had been amazing despite the challenging adjustments. There'd been some difficult weeks for Eli after we'd learned that Brennan had been raped by Memphis's ex. Eli had taken on the responsibility for making sure Brennan got what he needed, even though it had cost him emotionally. He was still dealing with trauma of his own rape at his stepfather's hands, especially since the man was adamantly fighting the charges and threatening to expose Eli's past as part of his defense. And that didn't even factor in the trouble we were having with Eli's stepbrother, Caleb.

Saying Caleb was a mess was an understatement. In short, the young man refused to interact with any of us. He and Eli's mother Mariana, were living in a condo about ten miles from us. Mariana had found work with a non-profit that supported veterans and their families, but she'd been struggling with Caleb from day one. He'd refused to go to therapy and even when we'd forced him to attend a session with Eli and Mariana, Caleb had merely sat there and stared at the wall. He'd barely spoken since his father had been arrested and we hadn't been able to make him go to school. Early on, Mariana had driven him to school each morning and watched him go in, but by the time she got home, the school had called to say Caleb hadn't shown up. He would eventually return home, but wouldn't say where he'd been and he wouldn't respond when we tried to talk to him. Mariana was at her wits end and so were Eli and I. And of course, Eli blamed himself for not having done something about his stepfather sooner.

I felt Eli stir against me and waited to see if he would wake up. He didn't, so I gently rolled him onto his back and then went to the bathroom to get a washcloth. I cleaned him off and then got him under the covers. As soon as I was settled next to him, Baby jumped up onto the foot of the bed and settled his big frame against Eli's feet. I wrapped myself around Eli and let my finger trail over his left ring finger, imagining how the band I'd bought him would look against his beautiful skin.

Ronan was right…Eli would say yes. And I was using Dom as an excuse…the only one really standing in the way of me finally getting everything I'd ever wanted was me.

But that was going to change.

Chapter 4

RONAN

"Hey," I said to Hawke as I reached out to shake his hand. I was surprised to find him waiting in the hospital lobby for me.

"Hey," he responded as he shifted nervously.

"Everything okay?" I asked.

Hawke nodded. "Seth said you were meeting him at 11 so I was hoping I could catch you before then."

"Yeah, sure," I said as I began walking towards the parking garage. "You mind giving me a ride and Seth can bring me back? We can talk on the way?"

Another nod and then Hawke fell in step next to me. He didn't even speak once we were on the road so I told him to head towards Queen Anne. "You're having lunch in Queen Anne?" Hawke asked.

Queen Anne was a suburb north of the city. It was the same neighborhood Hawke and Tate had recently bought a house in and that was one of the many reasons for today's appointment. "Seth and I are looking at a house there. It's actually just a few streets over from your place."

"Wow, really?" Hawke asked in surprise. "I knew you guys were thinking about moving to the city, but figured you'd end up downtown so you could be closer to work."

"Yeah, well, some things have changed in the last few days."

At Hawke's questioning look, I said, "Seth and I are looking into becoming foster parents for a couple of kids who don't have anyone."

Hawke actually pulled the car over to the side of the road and put it in park before turning to look at me. "Holy shit. Are you fucking with me?"

I smiled and shook my head.

"Why the hell am I just hearing about this now?" he asked.

"It's not a sure thing yet. Seth and I are still completing the process to become certified. If we get approved, we can get the kids in another week or so, but we want to lock down a house that's closer to the city. This house we're looking at is empty and if we like it, the realtor says the owner will let us rent it for the couple of weeks it takes to arrange the closing."

"What are the kids like?"

I felt my stomach clench. Seth and I had met the two children a few days earlier after we'd spent the better part of a day talking about whether we really wanted to pursue taking them in. I hadn't been at all surprised to find out that Seth would take a leave of absence from work to stay with the kids during the day if we got them. He'd been adamant that he could find someone to take over his responsibilities at the office and I'd known right then that Seth had found his purpose. He'd never been as passionate about his work as he'd been about giving these kids a better life. But I'd also known after we'd met the little girl and her brother that nothing about taking them in would be easy. They were as attached to one another as Seth had said they were and they hadn't wanted to interact with us at all. The only hint that there was even the possibility of making it work was when the little boy had fixated on Seth with his eyes until Seth had taken out his phone and handed it to him. He hadn't left his sister's side and she hadn't released her hold on him, but when the boy had gotten some kind of message on the phone that he couldn't get past, he'd carefully handed it to Seth expectantly so Seth could fix it before giving it back.

"The girl is around eight, maybe nine and the boy is two or

three. The authorities have no idea who they are or where they came from. The girl is deaf and neither of the kids speak, not even to each other...at least not that anyone's heard. They don't know if they even know how."

"Fuck," Hawke muttered and then he got the car moving.

"Zane is their advocate and says that because of the girl being deaf and possibly mute, he was having trouble finding a foster family to take them both together."

Hawke shook his head. "Wow, that's rough. If there's something Tate and I can do to help..."

"We'll let you know," I interjected. After a moment of silence, I said, "What did you want to talk to me about?"

"I...I have a favor to ask," Hawke began, but he wouldn't look at me. I knew asking for anything wasn't the norm for Hawke. Despite the support Seth and I had given him and Tate during Matty's treatment, Hawke was still a proud man and he wanted to be the one to take care of his family.

"We lost our wedding venue and I'm having trouble finding a new one. Tate and I are thinking of postponing-"

"Have it at our house," I cut in.

Hawke glanced at me and smiled and I realized that had probably been the question he'd been working up to. "We can clear out the sunroom at the back of the house. You'll still have the view of the water and mountains and there's enough room for everyone..."

"You wouldn't mind?" Hawke asked as he kept his eyes on the road. "Everything else is taken care of...the catering, the flowers..."

"We'd be thrilled," I responded.

Hawke nodded. "Thank you, Ronan...and not just for this..."

I put my hand on Hawke's upper arm and that seemed to be enough for him. We spent the rest of the drive talking about how Matty was adjusting to being home from the hospital. By the time we reached the address I gave him, I saw Seth's car in the driveway along with another car, likely the realtor's. "Thanks for the ride," I said.

"Keep us posted," Hawke called as I got out of the car and I nodded before trotting up the walkway to search out my husband so we could start yet another new chapter in our life.

Chapter 5

MAV

"So the reason I wanted to stop by-"

My words were cut off when a voice rang out from somewhere in the apartment, "Dom, are you here?"

"In here, baby," Dom called to his husband, even as his eyes stayed on me, his big hands wrapped around the coffee cup in front of him. I felt like a bug on a microscope slide with the way he was examining me. I reached for my own coffee and cursed inwardly at the slight tremor in my hand.

Fuck, I should have brought Matty like Ronan had suggested. He could have at least broken the damn ice.

But my pride had kicked in at the last minute and I'd told myself I was a grown ass man and didn't need a five-year-old fighting my battles. Only now I was wondering if a smarter man wouldn't have used every resource in his arsenal. Hell, at least I could have asked the kid if I could borrow his Spiderman doll for good luck or something.

I remained silent as I heard footsteps approaching and then the swing door to the kitchen was opening and Logan Barretti was striding through, his eyes searching out his husband's. It was the only time Dom took his eyes off of me and I watched as his entire countenance changed when he saw Logan. The other man leaned down to kiss Dom and I averted my eyes so I wouldn't intrude on the intimate moment.

"Hi," Logan murmured.

"Hi," Dom responded softly, sensually.

Would that be me and Eli in nine years? Would what we had now be as strong after nine years of sharing our lives?

Yes.

No question about it.

The thought gave me strength and I steeled my spine. I was good enough for these men…to be a part of their family for real.

"Hey, Mav," Logan said.

"Hi," I said with a nod.

"Mav has something he wants to talk to us about," Dom said as he linked his fingers with Logan's and urged him to sit.

Us?

Fuck. I'd prepared myself for one protective father, not two.

Both men looked at me expectantly, but before I could even get a word out, the swing door opened again. "Papa?"

Logan and Dom's four-year-old daughter strode into the kitchen and immediately crawled into Dom's lap. The family's German Shepherd, Sweetie, got up from where she'd been lying near my feet and ambled over to greet the little girl who immediately began petting the big dog.

"Did you have fun at pre-school today, baby girl?"

"Miss Valerie said I couldn't be a wise man in the pageant," the little girl pouted.

"How come?" Dom asked as he cuddled Sylvie against his chest.

"She said the wise men needed to be played by boys…she said I could be the In…In…"

"Innkeeper's," Logan supplied.

"The Innkeeper's wife." Sylvie straightened so she could look her father in the eye. "She said that I was a girl so I should play a girl part."

Dom ran his fingers over her dark hair and I could see the open love in his eyes. It pulled at something deep inside of me.

"Your Daddy and I will talk to Miss Valerie, okay?"

"Tell Papa what you said to Miss Valerie," Logan said and Dom glanced at him. A small smile graced Logan's lips and he gave Dom the slightest of nods.

"I told Miss Valerie that I knew the ABC song better than any of the boys and that I could run faster than all of them too. And none of the boys wanted to hold that furry spider…"

I must have shown my surprise at the last part of her statement because Logan glanced at me and said, "It was *Learn About Spiders* day a few weeks ago and someone brought in a tarantula."

I actually felt a shiver creep over my body at that. Sylvie turned to me and said, "It felt funny on my hand but it was nice. Papa and Daddy said I could maybe have one when I'm older." I nodded at Sylvie before she turned her attention back to Dom.

"What did Miss Valerie say?"

Sylvie snuggled against her father's chest again and calmly said, "She made me the leader."

"What?" Dom asked with a laugh.

"Apparently Miss Valerie says there is a strong possibility that there were four wise men." To his daughter he said, "But she didn't make you the leader."

Sylvie merely shrugged and then her gaze fell on me. Something flashed in her eyes and then she climbed off Dom's lap and left the kitchen, her pale blue eyes staying on me until she disappeared through the door, Sweetie at her heels.

"Sorry about that," Dom said with a laugh as his hand closed over Logan's again where it was resting on the table. "So what is it you wanted to talk to us about?"

I felt my body go hot as I leaned forward, but before I could even get a word out, another voice rang out. "Logan, Dom?"

"In the kitchen," Logan called.

I wanted to slam my head against the table when the swing door opened and more Barrettis flooded the kitchen. This time it was Dom's youngest brother Rafe and his husband Cade. "Hey," Rafe said as he leaned down to hug his brother. "Your secretary said you were working from home today so we wanted to stop by," Rafe said in a rush as he went around to hug Logan as well. Cade greeted both men as Rafe's eyes fell on me.

"Mav, hi. Wow, sorry, did we interrupt something?"

I began shaking my head when Dom said, "Mav stopped by to talk to me and Logan about something."

"Damn, sorry, our news can wait," Rafe offered, though his bright eyes said it really couldn't.

"No, please," I interjected and stood to go, but Cade put a hand on my shoulder.

"You can stay…you would have heard the news this weekend at family dinner anyway." Cade's eyes shifted to his husband and a big smile drifted across his mouth. "Tell them, baby."

Rafe smiled and nodded. His eyes dropped to his brother. "It's twins…a boy and a girl."

"What?" Dom whispered and then he was on his feet, pulling Rafe into his arms. More hugs followed and before I could even contemplate what was happening, more bodies filed into the kitchen. I immediately recognized Rafe and Dom's other brothers Ren and Vin along with one of Ren's partners, Jagger. Ren's service dog, Mick, trailed behind her owner.

"What's the big news little brother?" Vin said as he pulled Rafe into a quick hug. I lost track of things after that as Rafe and Cade shared the news about their surrogate's pregnancy and was planning to extricate myself from the celebration when Sylvie suddenly appeared at my side, hairbrush in hand. She didn't say anything as she stared at me expectantly and I couldn't help but smile as I reached down to lift her onto my lap. I pulled the tie holding my hair back and as soon as it was free, she began brushing it. It wasn't the first time the little girl had expressed her fascination with my hair.

The noise continued around us, but Sylvie didn't seem to notice. I suspected she was used to all the chaos considering the size of her family. I used the time to study the little girl. I suspected she was Logan's biological child based on her eyes and hair color, but she was clearly both her fathers' daughter. Would mine and Eli's child be the same way? Carry the DNA of one of us, but the traits of both? The idea of a son or daughter with Eli's dark eyes and unbreakable strength had me smiling. It would probably be a while before we could bring a child into our family, but the idea of it was no longer an uncertainty. We *would* have this someday. And we would have it as part of this bigger family of men and women who were so close that the news of impending fatherhood would be so important that they'd all rush to be together to share in the celebration of it.

It took me a moment to realize that the chaos around us had died down and I looked up to see all the Barretti men looking at me and Sylvie. Dom and Logan were once again sitting down, but their brothers and their partners were lined up behind them. It should have intimated the hell out of me.

It didn't.

"Dom, Logan, I have something I need to ask you," I finally said.

Vin was the one to pipe up and say, "We should probably go."

But I put up my hand before any of them could move. "Please stay," I said. "This pertains to Eli's family…his entire family."

I settled my eyes on Logan and Dom and said, "I love your son with all my heart. More than I ever thought it was even possible to love another person. He's put me first so many times and I want to spend the rest of my life doing the same for him. And I want this," I said as I motioned to the group of men. "*I* want this, I want Eli to have this and I want our children to have this." My eyes dropped to Sylvie and I ran my hand down her slim arm as her pretty blue eyes met mine and she smiled. "I want it all and I want to give it all to him."

It took me a moment to lift my eyes again. Every single pair of eyes was on me, but I didn't feel the same niggle of uncertainty I'd been feeling when I'd arrived. I was the man who could give Eli what he needed and I was worthy of him. These men had to know that…

The silence was broken when Cade suddenly said, "Pay up guys!" and held out his hand. Lots of grumbles followed as several of the men began pulling money out of their wallets and dropping it in Cade's hand.

"What the-" I managed to stop myself as I remembered Sylvie's presence.

"They had a bet going to see how long it would take you to ask Eli to marry you. Cade was the only one who said it would be less than six months," Rafe explained

I chuckled and shook my head as Cade shot me a smile. "I knew you were a goner the first time I saw you look at him." He cast his husband a glance and then grabbed his hand. "Let's leave these guys to it...we have some private celebrating to do." Rafe's eyes heated and then he was leaning down to hug Logan and Dom goodbye.

All of the men filed past me one by one giving me their private congratulations and dropping kisses on Sylvie's head. When it was finally just me, Dom, Logan and the little girl, I felt a little bit of apprehension return because both men hadn't said anything. "You...you guys didn't bet?" I finally asked.

Logan glanced at Dom before saying, "We had a private bet going."

"What was the bet?" I asked.

"Which one of you would propose to the other first," Dom said.

I stilled at that. "Has Eli said something?" I asked in disbelief.

"Eli asked Papa if he should buy you a ring," Sylvie chimed in as she continued to run the brush through my hair.

"Sylvie," Logan admonished. The little girl looked over her shoulder at her father. "Didn't you pinky swear Eli that you wouldn't tell anyone what you heard that day?"

"Oops, sorry Daddy," Sylvie whispered and I saw her face fall.

I tipped her face up and said, "Don't worry sweetheart, it was an accident. I won't tell him." Sylvie smiled and then lifted enough so she could whisper in my ear.

"He cried happy tears when Papa said you'd say yes."

I felt tears stinging my own eyes and I carefully gave Sylvie a squeeze. She sat back and said, "Are you gonna say yes?"

I managed a nod before I could find the words. "Yeah. Yeah I am."

"Can I throw the flowers?"

I laughed and said, "Yes, you can definitely be the flower girl."

Satisfied, Sylvie sat back and began working on my hair again.

"Mav," Dom finally said and I saw him lift Logan's hand to his mouth for a brief kiss. "Take care of our son and let him take care of you. That's all we ask."

Emotion clogged my throat and I barely managed to say, "I will. I swear it."

I forced back the tears that were threatening and focused my attention on Sylvie. "Sylvie, can you do me a favor and not tell Eli that I got him a ring?"

Sylvie studied me for a moment and then nodded. She held out her hand, fisted it until just the pinky was extended and said, "Pinky swear."

I took hold of her pinky with mine and said, "Pinky swear."

When she started brushing my hair again, I looked up at Logan and Dom and asked, "So which one of you lost the bet?"

Logan smiled broadly and cast a glance at Dom as color filled his cheeks. "Let's just say the way we bet…we both come out winners."

I rolled my upper lip to keep from laughing and forced my eyes back to Sylvie. "Fair enough," I said as a smile spread across my mouth.

Yeah, Eli and I would have this. Nine years or ninety…it didn't matter. We'd have it all.

I'd make sure of it.

Chapter 6

HAWKE

As I slid my arms around Tate's waist from behind, he automatically closed his hand over where mine were resting, but his eyes remained on the house across the street.

"This was what we wanted for him, remember?" I said gently against his ear.

"I know," he said with a nod. "I just…"

Tate shook his head and I held him tighter. "It's hard to let go even for one night." I felt him nod against me and then he was turning in my arms.

"Zane and Connor will let us know if he seems even the slightest bit off and Zane said he'd text us updates and pictures."

Tate chuckled and pulled back a little bit. "I'm going to be one of those parents, aren't I? The ones who can't let their kids go on the first day of school-"

"I'm going to be standing right next to you trying to force myself to let go of his hand," I cut in. Tate smiled and then pulled me down for a kiss.

"Our son's having his first sleepover," he said softly.

"And I'll bet he's having the time of his life."

Tate nodded and I led him over to the couch to sit down. Darkness was just starting to fall outside so the Christmas lights in our neighbors' yards were starting to turn on. I'd left our own lights on after Tate and I had managed to get them put up earlier in the day. I reached over to the end table to find the remote for the Christmas tree lights and turned them on. Tate curled against me as we silently admired our tree. Everything about the tree was fresh and beautiful including the new ornaments, shiny tinsel and bright lights, but my favorite part of it were the handmade ornaments Matty and Leo had spent an afternoon making. It had been Connor's idea to cut ornament shapes out of construction paper and decorate them with everything from markers to glitter to stickers. We had an array of snowmen and heavily colored, glitter-covered, ball-shaped ornaments, but the majority of the brightly colored works of art were plastered with all types of superhero stickers.

My phone buzzed and I immediately grabbed it.

"What is it?" Tate asked as he twisted around to get a look. He was hanging on to me when I opened the picture Zane had sent and we both smiled at the sight of Matty and Leo lying on their stomachs on the floor in front of the TV watching a cartoon. Storm was lying over the backs of both boys' legs. Tate took the phone and inhaled deeply and I finally felt his body relax against mine.

"You did it, baby," I said softly as I used my fingers to push a lock of his unruly hair behind his ear. "You gave him the life he deserved," I murmured as Tate looked up at me.

He shook his head and leaned in to kiss me. "*We* did, Michael. *We* gave it to him."

I shuddered when his mouth sealed over mine and he kissed me hungrily. My whole body caught fire as Tate crawled onto my lap and took control of my mouth. I let my hands close over his thighs as I held on to him while he tortured me with a mix of soft and deep kisses. "We should eat dinner first," I managed to say as Tate's hands skimmed over my shoulders, though food was the last thing on my mind.

"No we shouldn't," Tate whispered and then his tongue was dueling with mine. My dick was straining at my jeans and I could feel Tate's erection pressed up against my belly. Even though we made love every night and usually every morning before Matty woke up, I still couldn't get enough of this man. My need for him was absolute. The idea that he held so much power over me should have frightened me, but all it did was set me free.

As Tate worked my shirt over my head, I used one of my hands to search out my phone and managed to tuck it in my pocket before I grabbed Tate by the backs of his thighs and stood. He wasn't a light man by any means, but I wasn't willing to release him long enough to make the short walk to our bedroom. His legs wrapped around me and as I tore my mouth from his to watch where I was walking, his lips latched onto my neck. Fingers caressed my skin as I stumbled over a pair of shoes and narrowly managed to avoid a big dump truck toy in the hallway. When I reached our bedroom, I sought out Tate's mouth again, but I bypassed the bed and got us to the bathroom. It was only then that I released Tate and set him on his feet. He instantly began stripping as I got the shower going. I put my phone on the vanity before reaching for my pants, but Tate's eager fingers were already there. Only he didn't remove the pants beyond getting them past my swollen cock. And then he was on his knees and swallowing me down in one swift move.

"Shit," I muttered as I braced my hand on the shower door and watched my man suck me to the back of his throat. I used my other hand to thread my fingers through his hair and hold him in place as I ruthlessly used his mouth. Whimpers spilled from Tate's throat as I face-fucked him and then I yanked him to his feet and crushed our mouths together. I somehow managed to get the rest of my clothes off and once I had him in the shower, the hot water spraying over both of us, I turned him face first against the wall and roughly said, "Spread your legs."

Tate eagerly did as I asked, but I went a step further and kicked his legs even wider apart. He moaned at the rough treatment and I saw his hand reach for his flushed dick which I knew was leaking, even though I couldn't actually see the proof of that because of the water sluicing down his perfect skin. I grabbed Tate's hands and pressed them against the wall. "Leave them there," I said firmly and waited until he nodded. His cheek was pressed flat against the tile and he was breathing hard, but he didn't move even an inch as I took my time studying him. I let my hands skim over his tight ass before I slid a finger into his crease and played with his hole. Tate's lips parted and there was the slightest shift of his hips as he pushed against my probing finger, but he didn't move otherwise.

I lifted my finger to his mouth and waited and he instantly sucked it in and got it wet. The feel of his lips wrapped around the digit had my dick bobbing eagerly and I stepped forward and rubbed it against his ass as I whispered in his ear, "The wetter you get it, the faster it gets inside of you."

Tate squeezed his eyes closed and eagerly deposited as much spit on my finger as he could. I pulled my finger free of his mouth and worked it between our bodies until I found his hole. "You want this, baby?" I asked as I massaged him briefly.

"Yes, please," he begged shamelessly. "All of it!"

I gave him what he wanted and plunged my finger inside of his body in one swift move. The pleasure/pain had him crying out in relief and he shoved himself back on my finger as hard as he could. I used my hips to push him forward again and as I began finger-fucking him, I rubbed my dick between his legs to try to get some relief. I could feel his hard balls caressing my flesh and I knew he wouldn't last long.

I didn't bother with another finger because I knew neither of us could deal with that. I'd be lucky if I could even get a few strokes off at this rate. I pulled my finger free of his body and grabbed my cock as I reached for the lube that was sitting near where we kept the shampoo. I slathered my dick with it and then just dropped the bottle, too impatient to put it back where it belonged. I guided my cock to Tate's hole and then covered both his hands with mine and began to push into him.

"Michael," Tate cried out as my dick pierced his body. The sound of my name falling from his lips never failed to turn me on and I shoved several more inches into him. His ass gripped my flesh like a vise and I pulled back just a little before forcing more inside. Tate let out a wail of pleasure and then he was thrusting his ass onto my dick in an effort to get me all the way inside. I released his hands to grab his hips and I yanked him back as I drove forward until my balls slapped his ass.

"Yes!" Tate shouted and then he quickly said, "More!"

I pulled him back enough so he was folded over at nearly a forty-five-degree angle and then I began ramming into him as he braced his hands against the wall. He had no control like this, which I knew drove his passion even higher. "So fucking tight," I muttered as I pounded into him.

"Harder!" Tate nearly snarled and I felt one of his hands close over my thigh.

"Fuck," I snapped and I maneuvered us both to the floor of the shower, supremely grateful it was a walk-in shower and had plenty of room for us to work our bodies into whatever position we wanted. I fucked into Tate from behind several times as he begged and pleaded for more and then I pulled out of him and flipped him over so that he was on his back. It took just seconds to get back inside of him and then I covered his body with mine and kissed him hard. As much as I loved taking Tate from behind, this would always be my favorite position because I could see his eyes, taste his mouth, feel him clutch me in a hold that said he was never letting me go.

"Michael, please, I'm so close," Tate whispered as I slowed my moves.

I slid my hand between our bodies and began jerking him off to match the thrust of my hips. I could feel his ass pulsing around my cock and I knew it wouldn't take much more to send him over. I angled my hips just right and nailed his prostate as I gripped his cock hard.

Tate screamed my name so loud, I was sure the neighbors would hear, but I didn't give a shit as I slammed into him again, hitting him in exactly the same spot. A loud curse followed the next thrust and then he shattered and his inner muscles clamped down on my shaft. I kept my eyes on Tate as his orgasm consumed him, but I didn't slow my thrusts in any way. I did the opposite and rammed into him over and over as hard as I could, prolonging his climax and setting off my own. His hot cum kept sliding over my hand and between my fingers and as my own cock pumped inside of him, my release heating his flesh and mine, his orgasm went on and on. My own pleasure flung me into a chasm of darkness and then light and my muscles locked up tight. And then everything let go as more of my seed filled Tate's lush body and I sucked in a deep breath as I finally began the long fall back to earth. Tate's arms were there to welcome me as I collapsed on his slick, sticky chest. I could feel the hot water pounding my back, but I knew I was keeping the warmth from reaching Tate so I rolled us so I was on my back. Tate dropped his head to my chest as the water reached him and I wrapped my hands around the globes of his ass to keep myself inside of him for a little while longer.

"Michael," Tate whispered and I looked up at him. He didn't say anything else and he didn't need to. I saw it all.

We hadn't just given Matty the life he'd deserved…we'd given it to each other as well.

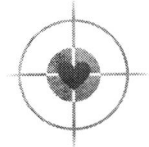

Chapter 7

RONAN

I wasn't sure what it was that woke me up, but it took me only seconds to realize that I was alone in bed and I automatically sat up and scanned the large bedroom. Seth had made a habit of leaving the light on in the bathroom each night so we could acclimate to finding our way around our new bedroom, so it was easy to see that the room was empty. I got out of bed and pushed the bathroom door open a little bit just to make sure he wasn't in there and then started for the bedroom door when I felt a cool rush of air wash over me. A glance to my left showed that the balcony doors were slightly open. I ignored the fact that I was wearing only a pair of briefs and went to the doors and opened them. I found Seth sitting on the ground, his back to the wall and a blanket wrapped around his body. His head was on his knees and Bullet was lying along one side of him with his big head buried in Seth's lap.

"Seth," I said softly as I crouched down next him and ran my fingers through his hair.

Seth inhaled sharply and lifted his head. There was enough light from the full moon to see the tears streaking down his face. "I'm sorry, Ronan," he whispered.

"For what, baby?" I asked as I dropped down next to him and pulled his upper body against my chest.

Seth shook his head and I just held him until he seemed to relax against me. "Come inside, Seth. It's too cold out here," I said. I put my arm beneath his elbow to help him, but he resisted.

"Please Ronan, I just need a few more minutes...the fresh air helps."

I nodded. "Okay, scoot forward a little."

He did as I said and I got behind him and sat down and then pulled him back against my chest. It took us a minute to get the blanket wrapped around us and then I slung my arms around his upper body and just held him. After a few minutes, I dropped my mouth to his ear and said, "What happened, baby? We had a good day today, didn't we?"

Seth nodded, but he didn't answer right away.

I thought back to the events of the day and tried to figure out if I'd missed something. It had been nearly three weeks since Seth had come to me about fostering the kids and we'd been in overdrive ever since. We'd moved into the house we'd looked at in Queen Anne a few days earlier and the Children's Protective Services social worker had been by the previous day to inspect it and had been pleased with the house itself as well as the neighborhood. Seth and I had completed the entire application process and required training and were just waiting for the call to see if we'd been approved or not. In addition to the training and endless paperwork we'd submitted, Seth and I had been spending a lot of time with both kids who Zane had been calling Jennie and Johnny Doe until their real names could be determined. All our visits had been supervised and had pretty much gone the same until today. Whereas the boy and girl had mostly ignored us during previous visits, Seth had managed to break down a big barrier today.

All our visits had taken place in a small play room full of toys, games and art supplies. The kids had spent each visit sitting quietly in one corner playing with building blocks or Legos...well, the little boy had played while the girl had kept her eyes on us the whole time. Seth and I had usually ended up sitting on the floor near them, but out of arm's reach, since any closer made the girl nervous and she'd refuse to release her hold on the boy to even let him play. The social workers and psychologists had seemed torn about how to break down the walls with the kids when Seth had suggested we try bringing Bullet to the session since the boy had shown interest in the dog's pictures on Seth's phone. They'd initially resisted since the dog technically wasn't allowed on the property and they weren't sure of the kids' reactions, but they'd finally relented.

Bullet had been a champ from the moment we'd walked through the door. The kids had been frightened at first so we'd sat on the opposite side of the room with Bullet and had just talked quietly to ourselves, keeping our backs to both kids. There'd been a mirror on one wall that was actually a two-way mirror and we'd used the reflection to keep an eye on the kids and Bullet. Once Seth had casually dropped Bullet's leash, the animal had started to work his way towards both children. But the dog had clearly sensed their apprehension because he'd taken his time dragging his body across the floor until he'd been within a few feet of them. When the little boy had gotten up and fought off his sister's hold to approach Bullet, Seth and I had held our breaths and we hadn't released it until the child had plopped down in front of the dog and started to run his hands over Bullet's face. Seth had carefully gotten up to join them both and miraculously, the boy hadn't moved. In fact, he'd clung to Bullet as if Seth was going to take him away. The little girl had tried to force her brother back and we'd all been stunned to hear her call out what we now guessed was the little boy's name.

Jamie.

The way the girl had said it had been confirmation that she was either partially or profoundly deaf. She'd followed up with frantic hand gestures that neither Seth nor I had understood despite the private sign language classes we'd signed up for. We'd learned later from one of the therapists watching the session that the girl had been telling the boy it wasn't safe. Jamie had signed back to his sister, though the therapist hadn't been able to catch what he'd said. And then his focus had been on Bullet…and Seth.

The girl had settled and watched the pair in silence from the corner. Seth had started showing Jamie some of Bullet's tricks and had even started teaching Jamie a few of the commands. And while Jamie hadn't spoken the commands, he'd quickly learned the hand gestures that went along with them. By the end of the hour, Jamie had been sitting in Seth's lap happily playing with the dog.

And Seth had never looked happier.

"I didn't want to leave them there," Seth finally admitted. "What if...what if we aren't approved?"

"We will be," I assured him. "Zane said we were excellent candidates and his recommendation holds a lot of weight."

Seth nodded.

"That's not all that's bothering you, is it?" I asked.

He shook his head. "I miss them so much, Ronan."

I instinctively knew he wasn't talking about the kids. "Your parents?" I asked.

He nodded. "They would have made the best grandparents," he whispered. "And Trace..."

My own throat closed up with emotion. I never gave thought to what would have happened with Seth and me if Trace were still alive because it didn't serve a purpose. But no matter how things would have ended up if Trace's life hadn't been stolen from him, Seth would have someday had kids who would have looked up to their uncle and were doted on by their grandparents.

"They're watching us right now, Seth. And I know how proud of you they are...of the man you've become and the father you're going to be." I dropped my lips to the back of Seth's neck and kissed him softly before settling my chin on his shoulder. "They're going to be our kids, Seth, whether it's for a few weeks until we find their family or it's for a lifetime because we're going to become their family. We're going to give Jamie and his sister the childhood you should have had...that we both should have had. We might not be able to give them grandparents, but we can give them a shitload of overprotective uncles."

Seth laughed and then he was turning in my arms. His arms went around my neck and he pressed his face against my neck. "I love you so much, Ronan."

"Me too, baby," I whispered. "Are you ready to go inside?"

Seth nodded and we climbed to our feet. He took my hand in his and led me back into the bedroom. I closed the balcony door behind Bullet, but before I could lead Seth back to bed, he was turning around and pulling me down for a kiss. His tongue stole hungrily into my mouth and I could feel his desperation rolling off of him in waves. But he wasn't just desperate for me.

I put my hands on each side of his face to hold him still so I could see his eyes. "Take what you need, baby."

The fact that a tear slipped from his eye told me his emotions were still right along the surface. He nodded and then he took my hand in his again. But instead of leading me to the bed, he urged me to an oversized plush armchair in the corner of the room. I sat and watched as Seth went to the bed to grab the lube from the nightstand. He was wearing a pair of thin pajama bottoms which he stripped off when he reached me. I would have expected him to be the one to fuck me, but when he coated his finger with lube and started prepping himself, I knew he needed something more. And he couldn't hold out long enough for me to get him ready the way I usually did.

Seth dropped to his knees between my spread legs and then reached for my briefs. I lifted my hips to let him pull them off of me and then his talented tongue was licking a path up my already hard shaft. I sighed and put my hand on his head just so I could have that connection with him as he pleasured me. He didn't linger too long before he swallowed me down and sucked on me hard. I didn't try to stifle the moan that fell from my lips, but I made sure not to thrust into his mouth the way I was tempted to do. There were days where one or both of us needed it rough or fast and there were other days where it was more about touching and kissing than actually getting each other off. Today was one of those rare days where Seth needed to be in complete control…not of me, but of what he needed from me. He needed to set the pace, he needed to determine the outcome.

Seth gave me a few more hard sucks before he pulled off and began slathering lube on my painfully sensitive cock. When he climbed up onto my lap, I helped steady him as he reached behind himself to position me at his opening. I didn't move as he began bearing down on me and it wasn't until my crown had breached him that he put both hands on my chest and let his head fall back. I could feel the tremor in his fingers as he dug them into me as more of my length filled him. I let my hands rest on his thighs as I tried to keep myself from slamming up into him.

It was slow going as Seth lifted a little before dropping down again. By the time I had bottomed out inside of him, I could feel my balls drawing up tight against my body. Seth held his position for several long seconds as his body adjusted to me and I hated that I couldn't see his eyes because he had them closed and his head was still thrown back. But I felt a crushing relief when he finally leaned forward and opened his eyes. They still looked pained, but they were bright with something else too…something I would never tire of seeing for as long as I lived.

His lips closed over mine as he began riding me. His moves were slow, but he took me as deep into his body as he could with each glide of his hips against mine. Our kisses matched his pace…slow, deep, unhurried. And the passion began to build in waves that grew larger and larger with every touch, every thrust, every kiss. Sweat slicked both our bodies as our rhythms synced up and I began to meet Seth's glides with answering thrusts. Within minutes, we were both desperate for more and Seth began rocking frantically against me and his hands held my face as he kissed me. He'd been letting these little whimpers fall from his throat when he'd first taken me inside of him, but I heard his cries of distress start to build as his need grew.

I knew he was trying to outrun the pain that had sent him out on that balcony and I was more than eager to take it away from him. I didn't ask permission before I wrapped one arm around him and used my other arm to lift up from the chair. I immediately took him to the floor, covering his body with mine, not letting our bodies separate for even a moment. I drove into him hard and he let a sharp cry of relief.

"Is this what you need, baby?" I asked softly.

Tears flowed freely down Seth's face again as he nodded. "Please," was all he said.

I pushed into him again, but instead of pounding into him to give him the orgasm he was waiting for, I kept fucking him with slow, deep thrusts. I didn't try to stem his tears, nor did I make an effort to wipe them away. He needed them as surely as he needed me to fill up those empty places inside of him that had sheared open today. He might have needed to be the one to start this encounter, but he needed me to finish it. I leaned down to kiss him softly as I slid my hips forward again, driving his ass higher. I linked our fingers together on the floor next to his head as I continued to drive into him. Keening cries began to escape his mouth and I stopped kissing him long enough to whisper, "Let it all go, my love."

Seth pulled his hands free of mine and locked them around my neck. He buried his face against my throat and just held on to me as I took him over the edge. I slid both my arms around his back and dug my fingers into his skin, pulling him as close to me as he could possibly be and then I took us both over. Seth let out a ragged cry as his orgasm ripped through him and I felt his teeth graze the skin where my shoulder met my neck. My own climax sent me flying and I dug my knees in the carpet as I pushed myself as deep into Seth as I could get and held there as I filled him. Seth's body jerked in my hold as his orgasm went on and on. I felt hot tears scalding my skin and I tightened my hold even more. When Seth's body finally relaxed as the pleasure began to ease, I wrapped an arm around his waist and held him to me as I sat up and rocked back onto my heels. Seth's legs went around me and he clung to me like a monkey as a fresh wave of tears dripped onto my skin. I held him like that for several minutes until his breathing finally slowed and his lips sought out mine. He used his hands to brush some of my damp hair off my forehead.

He looked like he wanted to say something, but he didn't. And I didn't need him to. I'd fixed some things for him, but some wounds just ran too deep to be completely healed. The best I could offer him was to take some of that pain when those wounds inexplicably tore open. He'd been doing the same for me from the moment I'd walked back into his life.

It was a long time before either of us moved. We showered together and just took pleasure in caring for each other's bodies and then we crawled back into bed. It took just minutes for us to fall asleep and Seth didn't even stir the following morning when my phone rang. I saw Zane's name on the caller ID and I kept my voice low when I answered it. I listened as Zane spoke and then I told him I'd call him back in a few minutes. I put the phone back on the nightstand and then curled myself around my husband.

"Seth, baby, wake up."

I felt Seth's fingers link with the ones I had resting on his stomach. He let out a little grunt so I leaned down to whisper in his ear. "They're ours, Seth."

The fingers playing with mine stilled and then Seth slowly rolled onto his back so he could look at me. "Really?" he said softly, his mouth turning up into a smile.

"Really," I said as I brushed my mouth over his. "Are you ready for this?"

Seth nodded and then he wrapped his arm around my neck to pull me down for another kiss. "I'm ready."

◆

"Are you guys ready?" Seth asked as he knelt in front of Jamie and his sister and double-checked to make sure both kids' jackets were buttoned up. Jamie nodded, but his sister didn't react in anyway…she merely clung to her brother's hand. Her other hand was resting on Bullet's neck.

It had been three days since we'd gotten the call that we'd been approved as foster parents for Jamie and his sister, and Seth and I had been frantically running around to get everything together to bring them home. We'd already had some of the basics like furniture for their rooms, but we hadn't wanted to get things like toys until we were sure they'd be coming home with us. We'd also gone each day to visit the kids and we'd taken Bullet along to continue to act as an icebreaker. Jamie had instantly left his sister's side at the sight of Bullet on the first day and he hadn't hesitated to crawl into Seth's lap again to play with the dog. His sister had been a slightly harder nut to crack, but she'd finally given in and interacted with the dog as well, though she'd steered clear of me and Seth. At this point, the only things connecting us to the little girl were Jamie and Bullet, but that was enough.

Neither kid had spoken beyond Jamie saying Bullet's name once. We suspected Jamie was capable of speaking, but chose not to. We were hopeful that with time that he'd open up to us and tell us as much as he could about himself and his sister, primarily her name. The pair were definitely communicating via sign language, but only enough for Jamie to tell his sister the dog was nice and she shouldn't be scared. When we'd explained to both of them yesterday - both verbally and using one of the therapists who knew sign language – that they were coming to stay with us at our house for a while, neither kid had reacted either negatively or positively.

I'd ended up talking to the hospital about postponing my joining the staff for a few months until my new family was settled and they'd been understanding and had told me there'd be a place for me whenever I was ready. Neither Seth nor I were expecting it to be an easy transition, but we'd both grown so attached to the children that we knew we'd do whatever it took to make it work. And if CPS happened to find the kids' family at some point, we'd accept it and find a way to live with whatever time we'd been able to have them for.

I watched as Seth took Jamie's free hand in his and I felt my heart pound painfully in my chest at the sight. Not only because of the pure joy in my husband's eyes, but because he just looked so right with both kids.

"All set?" I asked him as I grabbed Bullet's leash. I was on the dog's left side and Jamie's sister was on his right. She was resting her casted arm on Bullet's neck and her right hand was clutching Jamie's hand.

Seth nodded and I felt the emotion clog my throat at the sight of the smile that spread across his lips. Zane was behind us talking to the woman who'd been assigned to oversee the kids' case. I glanced over my shoulder at him and saw him nod and then he was taking a folder from the woman and he began leading the way out the door. He held the door for us and we filed out one by one.

The group home was actually a very large house in a small neighborhood on the city's south side. The neighborhood wasn't terrible, but it was pretty run down and we'd ended up having to park in the small lot next to the house. Seth led the way down the steps, mindful of the kids as they navigated them while I made sure Bullet didn't inadvertently bump into the little girl holding on to him.

So none of us noticed the figure until it was too late.

Bullet's snarl was what caused me to snap my head up just in time to see a gun aimed directly at me. "Don't move!" the person shouted in a high-pitched voice. The register was too high for an adult man's voice, but I couldn't tell if the assailant was a young man or woman because the hoodie was covering most of their face.

We'd just reached the bottom of the step when the order had been called out and I saw Seth instantly step in front of Jamie. I sensed Zane's presence behind me and hoped to God he was able to reach his phone without alerting our assailant.

"If you want money, I've got some," I said as I subtly stepped around Bullet so I could block the little girl. But before I could take another step, Jamie's sister cried out and pulled free of Jamie and began running forward. My instincts kicked in and I grabbed her by the waist to stop her. I'd managed to hang on to Bullet at the same time since I didn't want to risk him getting shot if I could diffuse the situation with words. I'd long ago stopped carrying a gun, so I knew the dog would be our only hope if I couldn't talk the assailant down.

"Let her go!" the figure shouted as the little girl struggled in my grasp.

"Willow!" I heard Jamie shout and I saw him trying to pull free of Seth's hold.

"I said let her go!" the figure shouted again and the little girl in my grasp began crying out to the figure. I realized the girl was saying the same name Jamie had said and it hit me then that the assailant was in fact a girl and that she clearly knew Jamie and his sister.

Between Bullet's snarls and wanting to use my body to block Seth and Jamie, I lost my hold on Jamie's sister and she flew down the rest of the walkway into the young woman's arms. The impact knocked the girl's hoodie loose to reveal short blonde hair that fell just below her chin. My heart stopped as I realized she wasn't even a young woman…she couldn't have been more than fourteen years old. My eyes fell to her gun and I struggled to get a better look at it as she waved it wildly around.

"Let him go!" she yelled as she held on to the little girl with her free hand. She pointed the gun at Seth, but her eyes were on Jamie.

"Willow!" Jamie screamed again and then all hell broke loose and I was powerless to stop it.

Out of the corner of my eye, I saw the group home's security guard returning from his cigarette break. As soon as he drew his gun I yelled, "Don't! Her gun is a fake!" but it was too late and the man pulled the trigger just as Willow turned in his direction. The sound of the gun was deafening and I watched in horror as the impact sent her flying backwards. The little girl went down with her and I screamed in denial as I saw blood spray against the side of the white car just behind both girls.

I frantically hurried to them and dropped down next to them. Jamie's sister was crying as she tried to right herself to a sitting position and I grabbed her and scanned her quickly. As much as I wanted to comfort her, I knew she wasn't the one who'd been hit so I yelled, "Zane! Take her!"

Zane appeared at my side a second later and his big hands closed around the girl's waist and he was lifting her in his arms and pulling her away. I ignored her and Jamie's cries as I focused on Willow.

Blood was quickly turning her hoodie and the light blue shirt beneath it bright red. The bullet had hit her on her right side and while she was still conscious, the young girl was gasping for air. I dropped my head to her chest to listen and felt a sliver of relief that neither of her lungs appeared to be collapsing and I realized she'd likely just had the wind knocked out of her when she'd fallen.

"You're gonna be okay Willow," I said as I gently rolled her to her side so I could see if the bullet had exited her body.

Tears were flowing down her face. "Jamie…Nicole," she gasped.

"They're fine," I said as I eased her on her back again. "Not hurt."

"Sir, I need you to step back."

I barely spared the security guard a glance. "I'm a doctor," I bit out as I began ripping Willow's clothes so I could see the wound.

"I need to secure the suspect," the guy said. "Please step away."

I ignored the man so I could focus, but when he leaned down with a pair of zip tie cuffs, intent on restraining the girl, I snagged him by the shirt and said, "If you lay one fucking hand on her, I'm going to rip it off."

The man blanched, but he didn't back off. "I need to secure-"

I didn't even let him finish. Instead, I grabbed his gun from his holster and pointed it at him. "Back. The. Fuck. Off," I snarled and he instantly put his hands up and backed away. I lowered the gun and quickly released the clip and emptied the chamber and threw both the clip and the bullet in the bushes behind me. I snatched up the girl's fake gun which was still lying next to her and slid it and the security guard's empty gun under the car next to us and then continued working on Willow. She was still awake, but her eyes were starting to glaze over.

"Hang in there, Willow," I said as I finished ripping her shirt. I heard sirens in the distance and hoped like hell it was the paramedics.

"I…I promised them," Willow whispered as her eyes began to drift shut.

"Willow, honey, open your eyes," I demanded as I gave her a little shake. She opened them again and then turned her head slightly so she could see both kids who I could hear frantically crying behind me.

"What did you promise them?" I asked as I tried to keep her awake. The wound was bleeding heavily and I was helpless to do anything but apply pressure to it. "Willow, what did you promise them?" I asked the girl again.

"We...we'd...."

"Open your eyes, sweetheart," I demanded. "Tell me about the promise!"

Willow managed to open her eyes again, but I knew I wouldn't be able to keep her talking because already her words were slurring. "Family," she murmured tiredly. "Always a family."

"You promised them you'd always be a family?"

But she didn't answer me and when her head lolled to the side, I dropped my head to her chest and listened and then checked her pulse. "Fuck," I snapped and then I glanced over my shoulder. "Zane!" I yelled and he was there at my side. I had no idea what had happened to Nicole, but she wasn't with him which I was glad for. "I need to do CPR," I said. "Keep pressure here," I said as I grabbed his hands and made him press down hard on the bullet wound. I began chest compressions and sent out a silent prayer of thanks when the ambulance rolled up a moment later.

My eyes locked with one of the paramedics and I recognized him from the time Brennan had been shot the previous summer.

"We gotta stop meeting like this, Doc," he murmured without humor as he began inserting an IV while his partner got the gurney ready.

"Yeah," I muttered.

"You know this one too?" he asked as his partner reached us and they got the gurney into position.

"Yeah," I said. "She's family."

Chapter 8

MEMPHIS

"Memphis, over here," Tristan said as he tugged on my hand before I could even talk to the woman behind the desk. I turned to where he was pointing and saw Ronan, Seth, Zane and two little kids sitting in one corner of the busy waiting room.

"Ronan," I called softly because it looked like both kids were asleep. The little boy was tucked up against Seth's side and the girl was pressed up against the boy.

Ronan got up and leaned down to say something to Seth who nodded. Both men looked like shit.

"I'm gonna go sit with Seth," Tristan said to me as his eyes shifted back and forth between Ronan and Seth. I nodded and brushed a kiss over his lips.

"Can you text Brennan and let him know where we are?" I asked. Tristan and I had been grocery shopping when I'd gotten the call from Ronan to meet him at the hospital. Brennan had been in class at the time so we hadn't wanted to disturb him, but he would be on his way home now and I knew he'd want to be here to support our friends.

"Yeah," Tristan said. He reached out to hug Ronan as he passed him on the way to where Seth was sitting. Ronan returned the embrace and then he made his way to my side and motioned to a section of the waiting area where there weren't as many people.

"Thanks for coming," he said, his voice sounding rough.

"How's the girl?" I asked. Ronan had given me enough information over the phone that I knew the basics of what was going on.

"She's going to be okay. They're closing her up right now. The bullet nicked an artery but luckily didn't do any other major damage."

"Thank fuck," I muttered as I shook my head.

"Listen, I need you to stay here with Seth and the kids and keep an eye on them. There was an…altercation…between me and the guy who shot the girl. I rode over in the ambulance so I'm guessing the cops will be here soon."

"What kind of altercation?" I asked.

Ronan lifted his eyebrows just slightly and I shook my head. As if on cue, Declan Barretti appeared and immediately zeroed in on Ronan. He glanced briefly at Seth and Tristan and I saw Tristan get up and go to him. The big man embraced his nephew and then said something softly in his ear and Tristan glanced at me and Ronan worriedly. But he returned to his seat. I saw Zane and Declan acknowledge each other before Declan made his way to us. I automatically tried to stand in front of Ronan, but Ronan put his hand on my arm to stop me and shook his head. Declan and I hadn't gotten off to the best start with each other the previous summer when Brennan had been shot, but we'd managed to make peace after I'd begun seeing both of his nephews. And he'd been instrumental in dealing with the fallout from Brennan, Tristan and Tanner's abduction.

"Ronan," Declan said with a nod and then his eyes shifted to me. "Unclench Wheland," he said with a slight smirk.

"Fuck you, Declan," I said, though there was no real anger behind the words. I knew the guy was just doing his job. I'd seen the man with his partners and his daughters and knew he was actually a good man.

"If we could do this outside, I'd appreciate it," Ronan said as his eyes shifted to Seth. I didn't miss the tension in Seth's gaze and I guessed if he hadn't had the kids to worry about, he would have been at Ronan's side.

"Here's fine," Declan said and I felt my gut clench.

"Declan-" I began, ready to ask the guy nicely not to arrest Ronan in front of his husband and new family.

Declan put his hand up to stop me from speaking, but kept his eyes on Ronan. "Zane told me what happened when he called me. I've smoothed things over with the security guard and he's not pressing charges for that little trick with the gun," he began.

"Why not?" Ronan interrupted. Leave it to Ronan to not just accept what the man was saying.

"I may have reminded him that it wouldn't look so good on the six o'clock news that not only had the man shot a fourteen-year-old girl and put another one at risk with his actions," – Declan's eyes shifted to where the little girl was asleep on the bench – "he'd also interfered with the life saving measures being taken to help the girl and then allowed himself to be disarmed by a civilian." Declan added a slight drawl to the last word. Yeah, the man knew Ronan was anything but your average guy.

"Declan-" Ronan began, but then fell silent. He clearly hadn't expected the turn of events.

"Can you do me a favor next time, Ronan?" Declan asked.

"There won't be a next time," Ronan responded, but Declan just tilted his head knowingly. "What?" Ronan finally asked.

"Next time just knock the fucker out cold…saves me a lot of paperwork."

With that, Declan turned and motioned to Zane who got up and joined us. "I did the search you asked for," Declan said to Zane.

"What search?" Ronan asked.

"I asked Declan to search for any missing persons reports for the kids," Zane said. "All the searches we did before were for two kids, not three, and we didn't have their names." Zane paused before saying, "Ronan, I'm sorry, it's my job-"

"It's okay," Ronan interjected and his eyes shifted to Declan. "What did you find?"

"They're runaways. They were living with their aunt and uncle in Portland after their parents died in a car crash earlier this year. The oldest, Willow, took the kids while the aunt and uncle were both at work almost three months ago," Declan said.

"Why?" I asked. All three men looked at me and I clarified, "Why did they run away?"

"The aunt said Willow had some mental problems and was convinced her parents were still alive. They grew up around here so they think Willow brought them here to find their parents."

Declan shifted his eyes back to Ronan. "The aunt and uncle are on their way here. They should be here in an hour or so."

Zane shook his head. "We'll confirm that they're the kids' legal guardians Ronan…" Zane began before glancing at where Seth and the kids were sitting, but he didn't finish his sentence and he didn't need to. We all knew what the turn of events meant.

"Thanks," Ronan said dully and then he began heading towards Seth. I knew what was coming and I could see Seth did too because his fear-laden eyes were on his husband and his grip on the little boy still asleep against his side tightened. Tristan got out of the chair Ronan had been sitting in and came to my side. I automatically put my arm around him.

"Seth," Ronan began but Seth shook his head and I could see he was struggling to hold it together.

"Don't," was all he said and then he dropped his head to Ronan's chest.

"I'm sorry, baby," Ronan murmured and Seth nodded. I heard a muffled sob escape his throat, but he managed to hold it together.

"Let's go get them some coffee," Tristan said as he leaned into me. I nodded and took his hand. We searched out the cafeteria and got some coffees, a couple of bottles of milk for the kids and some snacks and took everything back to the waiting room. Ronan and Seth thanked us, but didn't show any interest in the coffee. The little boy was awake and playing with Seth's phone, but the girl was still asleep.

"Seth, is there anything we can do?" Tristan asked as he knelt down in front of him.

Seth shook his head. "Um, Zane just left to take Bullet to Hawke and Tate's house so we're okay, thanks."

"Jamie! Nicole!"

We all turned our heads at the sound of a woman's voice.

"Oh thank the Lord," a woman in a long red coat sputtered as she hurried towards us. She was nearly as tall as the man behind her and thin as a stick. Her hair was twisted into a severe knot on the top of her head and her makeup looked like it had been applied with a paint roller. I guessed her to be in her early forties at the most and she was professionally dressed in an expensive looking pants suit. The man behind her was also dressed in what I figured was a designer suit. His face was drawn into a severe expression.

Ronan stepped in front of the woman before she could reach the kids and her husband immediately moved to her side.

"Who are you?" the man asked as he pulled the woman back just a little.

"My name is Ronan Grisham-" Ronan began.

"The foster parents," the man cut in. His eyes shifted to Seth and the kids. The girl was still asleep but the boy had actually buried his face in Seth's armpit as if trying to hide from the man. "I'm Gene Teasdale. This is my wife, Alana," he said as he motioned to the woman next to him. "We're supremely grateful that you were willing to step up to watch out for these guys," – the man motioned to the two kids – "and we understand you're the reason Willow is alive." The man extended his hand. "Thank you…we've been so worried about them since they disappeared."

Ronan hesitated before finally taking the man's hand and I could tell he was sensing the same thing as me…the words coming out of the guy's mouth were the right ones but there was something just…off.

"Jamie, we missed you," Alana said softly as she dropped down in front of the bench, but the little boy didn't acknowledge her except to burrow farther into Seth's hold. Alana turned her attention to the little girl. Ronan had told me the girl, Nicole, was deaf so I wasn't surprised when the woman shook her awake instead of calling her name.

Nicole was groggy at first and my heart went out to her when I took in her tear-stained face. Her long blonde hair hung in a messy tangle and she pushed it from her eyes before she settled them on Alana and then Gene. Her eyes flew open and she scrambled to her brother's side. I could see her fingers moving lightening fast as she looked at Seth and I realized she was signing.

"Enough of that nonsense!" Gene snapped and he suddenly grabbed Nicole by her uninjured arm and pulled her off the bench. The little girl gasped and went completely still.

"Hey," Ronan snarled and then he was shoving Gene back.

The man bristled, but released the child. "She knows how to talk, but she won't if you don't force her."

"Touch her again-" Ronan warned, his eyes going dark.

"Ronan!"

I saw Declan approaching, a cup of coffee in hand. He put it down on a side table, presumably so he could keep his hands free. It wasn't a good sign.

"Are you Mr. and Mrs. Teasdale?" Declan asked as he stepped between the two men. Nicole still hadn't moved and she was too far from Seth for him to reach her without moving Jamie so Tristan was the one who actually dropped down next to her and settled his hand on her back and began rubbing soothing circles on it.

"We are," Gene said. "Are you Captain Hale?"

Declan nodded. "Did you bring the paperwork I asked for?"

The man nodded and pulled a folded document from his suit jacket and handed it to Declan. Declan scanned it and then nodded to Ronan. I saw the disappointment flood through my friend.

"Dr. Grisham, she's awake," a young nurse said as she approached our group. "Dr. Sterns says you can see her now...she's in room 304. If you'd like to come with me..."

Ronan stepped forward, but Gene put his arm out. "I'd like to see my niece, please," he said to the confused young woman. "Alone," he added as he looked at Declan. Declan glanced between him and Ronan and then nodded at the nurse.

"Right this way, sir," she said uncomfortably and motioned towards the hallway to the right of the waiting room.

"Alana, take the kids to the car." Gene's cool gaze fell on Ronan. "We'll be taking them to a hotel so they can get some rest." With that, the man followed the nurse.

Pain lanced through me as I saw Seth hug Jamie tightly before forcing the little boy away from his body so he could look at him.

"This is fucked up, Declan," I said.

"My hands are tied," the man responded and I could see he wasn't happy about it at all.

"Come children, we should go," Alana said as she reached for Nicole's hand. But Nicole jerked away from her and then she was pushing into Tristan's arms. I could hear her crying and I watched as Tristan wrapped his arms around her and lifted her enough so he could sit on the bench with her on his lap.

Ronan was leaning over Seth whispering something to him when I heard Tristan say, "Memphis."

I looked over at him and saw him holding out the hand he'd used to support the girl's bottom as he'd been lifting her. He lifted her enough so that I could see a large, wet stain between her legs.

"Ronan," I said as I kept my eyes on the way Nicole clung to Tristan. She was shaking violently. Ronan's eyes fell on the wet mark and he stiffened. His hard gaze shifted to Alana. But she refused to meet his look.

"Come on, Jamie," she said loudly and then she tried to grab the little boy's arm. But Seth snatched him up and Declan put his hand on Alana's arm. He too had seen that the little girl had wet her pants – and the stain definitely hadn't been there before her aunt and uncle had arrived.

Ronan was moving before anyone could even say anything and I followed after him. It seemed to take forever to find room 304 and when we did, I immediately noticed that the privacy curtain had been drawn. Ronan was several steps ahead of me, so by the time I followed him into the room, he was already putting his hands on Gene who was leaning over the girl in the bed. He ripped the man off the girl and I heard her let out a big gasp. I could see that her throat was red where the fucker had been holding on to her.

I took pleasure in the sound of flesh striking flesh as Ronan

A Protectors Family Christmas

slammed his fist into Gene's face. I shielded the girl so she wouldn't see the blood spray from the man's mouth as some of his teeth went flying. But I quickly realized the girl was having trouble breathing. "Ronan!" I shouted and, luckily, my voice got through to him. "There's something wrong!" I said.

Ronan dropped the prone man to the floor just as Declan came flying into the room. Ronan rushed to the bed and then he was hitting a red button just above the girl's bed. I stepped back as several medical staff came rushing into the room and watched as Ronan grabbed an oxygen mask and put it over the girl's face.

"Willow, I need you to take deep breaths, okay?"

The girl was shaking her head violently and I heard Ronan say to one of the nurses, "She's having an asthma attack. Epinephrine," he ordered. The nurse glanced at what I could only assume was the girl's actual doctor who looked like he was checking the surgical incision on her side.

"Do it," the doctor said quickly.

The nurse drew up the medication as Ronan talked calmly to Willow. He took the syringe when she handed it to him and he inserted it into the IV port on the girl's arm. "Have another one on standby," he said as he handed the syringe back to the nurse and then took the stethoscope she offered him and used it to listen to the girl's breathing.

It took several long minutes before things quieted and the girl finally seemed to be able to breathe more normally. Declan had removed a handcuffed Gene from the room and by the time I got to the waiting room to update Seth and Tristan, Alana was in the custody of a uniformed police officer, though she wasn't cuffed. Tristan and Seth were sitting next to each other, still holding onto both kids and I saw that Brennan had joined them and that he had his arm around Tristan's shoulders. I grabbed a passing nurse and said, "Do you have something she can wear?" I asked as I motioned to Nicole.

The nurse saw the obvious wet stain and said, "I'll get something."

My eyes connected with Brennan's and he smiled at me. As

always, I felt my insides jump and it took everything in me not to go over and kiss both my men. Instead, I gave him a look promising I'd greet him properly later and then went to find Declan to make sure Alana and her shit bag of a husband weren't ever getting their hands on any of the kids again.

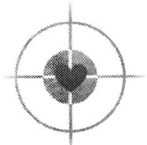

Chapter 9

MAV

"Mav, come on in," Declan said as he waved me over before I could even tell the officer sitting near the entrance to the department my name. Trepidation washed over me as I entered his office and he shut the door behind me.

"Thanks for coming down so fast," Declan murmured as he sat down behind his desk and motioned for me to sit across from him. "I know Eli's got his finals this week," he began. I nodded.

"He's taking one right now," I managed to get out.

Declan nodded. "I wanted to talk to you before I call Mariana."

I managed another nod. "Where is he? Is he okay?"

"He's safe," Declan acknowledged and I felt a wave of relief wash over me. Declan hadn't given me any details when he'd called other than to say it was about Caleb and I needed to come to the station right away. My heart had been in my throat the entire drive.

"He's here," Declan added. "One of my officers found him on the Aurora Bridge about an hour ago. He was drinking, but a breathalyzer showed he wasn't legally drunk."

"Okay," I said, though my throat felt tight because the tone of Declan's voice said there was more and it wasn't good.

"I know you aren't from around here," Declan said. "That

bridge…it has a reputation."

"What?" I asked in confusion. How the fuck did a bridge have a reputation?

"The bridge is one of the few in the area that has pedestrian access…"

"I don't understand," I admitted, still completely clueless.

"The bridge has been a popular location for jumpers in the past."

I felt my heart beat painfully in my chest at that and heat flooded my entire system. "What?" I whispered, praying I'd heard the man wrong.

"There were so many suicides in the late nineties and early two thousands that the city erected an 8-foot fence to deter people from jumping. It's been effective, but people still try on occasion. A few sections of the fence are being replaced because there's something wrong with the steel that was used to construct it. Caleb was standing in front of one of the sections where the fence had been taken down to make way for the repairs."

"Oh my God," I whispered as the pain in my chest exploded.

"He listened to the officer's orders to step away from the side, but the officer said he seemed to hesitate…he couldn't be sure but he said it was just a feeling he had. When he called into the station to ask if he should take the kid to the hospital as a precaution, I found out it was Caleb and had him bring him here. He's in an interview room and there's an officer watching him."

I dropped my face into my hands and shook my head in disbelief. This couldn't fucking be happening. "Did he say anything?" I asked.

"No, he refused to talk to the officer or me. He keeps asking for someone named Jace."

"What?" I said as I snapped my head up.

"Do you know who he is?"

I nodded. "He's the guy we had watching Caleb in D.C." I didn't add that Jace was the one who'd gotten Caleb out of the psychiatric hospital his father had stashed him in. Or that I suspected Caleb was harboring feelings for the older man.

I hadn't spoken to Jace after he'd left earlier in the summer and Caleb hadn't once asked about the man. But clearly, Eli's stepbrother was still stuck on whatever connection he'd forged with Jace.

"Fuck," I muttered as I realized I had no idea how to proceed. We'd been so sure Caleb would come around, especially once the shit with his father died down and the man began serving his sentence. But I hadn't seen this coming. And it was going to fucking tear Eli apart.

"Can I see him?" I asked.

Maybe there was some reasonable explanation for this. Maybe if I just talked to the young man, I could get the answers I needed.

"Yeah," Declan said and I followed him from the office. He led me to a room at the far end of the space. "There's a two-way mirror in there. If you don't mind, I'm going to watch from the other side," the man said and I nodded.

Declan opened the door and motioned to the young male officer standing in the corner of the room. Caleb was pacing back and forth along the far wall. His eyes shifted up to meet mine, but he just shook his head and kept walking. I was stunned at how agitated he was. In the past few months he'd been so withdrawn and quiet, but now he was like a caged animal.

The officer and Declan left, closing the door behind them.

"Caleb-"

"No!" he shouted. "I don't want to talk to you! I want Jace! He fucking promised me!"

"What did he promise you?" I asked as a wave of uncertainty went through me. I'd worked with Jace several times and I knew him to be a good guy. But if he'd led Caleb on in some way...

But Caleb ignored me and kept walking back and forth in the confined space. "Caleb, why were you on that bridge?"

Caleb slowed and then turned to face the wall, putting his back to me. "Mav, please let me talk to Jace."

I saw his shoulders hunch and I could tell he'd wrapped his arms around himself. I pulled out my phone and dialed Jace's number. I kept my eyes on Caleb and when Jace answered I said, "Jace, Caleb wants to talk to you."

I didn't give Jace a chance to answer because Caleb had turned around. The hopeful look in his eyes tore at my heart and I was reminded of how young he really was and how fucked up his life had become. I put the phone on the table and said, "I'll be outside. Just knock on the door when you're done."

Caleb nodded and then his unsteady hand was reaching for the phone.

I left the room and immediately sought out the room next to it. Declan glanced at me as I entered. I could hear Caleb's shaky voice through the intercom as he whispered, "Jace?"

I probably should have felt guilty about listening in on his conversation, but I didn't. Not in the least. The young man's life was on the line. I wasn't playing games anymore and I sure as hell wasn't going to worry about my conscience. There was of course no way to hear what Jace was saying, but it wasn't important. I'd talk to Jace to get his side of things when Caleb was done.

"No," Caleb said softly and then I saw him sink into one of the chairs and support his head with his free hand. "He's gonna get out, Jace," Caleb whispered, his voice catching in his throat.

I glanced at Declan. We both knew who Caleb was talking about. His piece of shit father.

Caleb was silent as Jace spoke and then he shook his head. "I…I can't sleep. I can't think. I keep seeing Nick…"

Caleb's voice dissolved as a sob tore from his throat. "Jace… please…I need you."

Using his sleeve to wipe at his tears, Caleb listened to Jace talk for a while, nodding every once in a while. Whatever Jace was saying seemed to help somewhat because Caleb sucked in a couple of deep breaths.

"Okay," he said quietly and then he got up and went to the door and knocked on it. I left the observation room and hurried back to the interview room. Caleb stepped back from the door and handed me the phone. "He wants to talk to you," was all he said and then he went to sit down again.

I put the phone to my ear and said, "Yeah?"

"I'm on my way," was all Jace said before he hung up on me.

I COVERED ELI'S HAND WITH MINE AS HE STRUGGLED TO REIN IN THE tears that had been falling from the moment I'd told him why Caleb was at our house. I hadn't known what to say to Mariana about why Caleb was spending the night with us so I'd lied and said Caleb had asked to spend some time with Eli. I felt like shit for keeping the truth from the woman, but I needed to focus on Eli and he and I needed to make some decisions together about Caleb's future.

Because Caleb had clearly become too much for Mariana to deal with on her own.

"Do you think he was really going to do it?" Eli asked.

"I don't know," I said honestly. "I'm hoping Jace can find out for sure, but I think we need to go forward thinking it's a very real possibility."

Eli shook his head and wiped at his eyes. I got up and snagged some paper towels for him. He dried his face and then straightened. "I'll take a leave from school."

"Nuh-uh," I said as I shook my head. "Absolutely not."

"He's going to need someone watching him and my mom can't do this on her own..."

"She won't have to," I responded before Eli could continue. "I think he should come stay with us for a while. I've already talked to Memphis about me continuing the operations side of things which means I'll be working from home indefinitely..."

"No, Mav, I can't ask that-"

I leaned over and kissed him hard to silence him. "You're not asking. He's my family too, Eli. And this is what family does for each other."

I felt Eli's hand come up to wrap around the back of my neck and he pressed his forehead against mine. "It's gonna get easier, right?" he asked.

I skimmed my lips over his and whispered, "The hard part was everything that came before we found each other."

Eli nodded and then he was pushing into my arms. I wrapped my arms around him and felt the tension in my body ease. I was still scared shitless about everything we were facing, but there was one thing that wasn't even a question mark for me anymore.

"Eli, I need to ask you something-"

"Yes, Mav. The answer is yes." His whispered words in my ear had my whole system seizing up tight. I pushed him back a bit so I could see his face.

"You know?" I asked in disbelief. "Who...who told you?"

Eli's hand skimmed over my cheek. "You did," he said softly.

I shook my head, but couldn't find any words.

"I'm thinking you made the decision to ask me a few weeks ago, right?"

I nodded stupidly. "How?"

"You started looking at me differently...you just suddenly seemed so unsure of yourself. I...I thought maybe you weren't sure about us so I went to talk to Dom. I thought maybe if I asked you-"

I cut him off with a kiss. "I'm sorry, baby...I *was* having doubts, but not about you or us..."

Eli put his thumb over my lips to stop me. "It's yes, Mav. It's been yes from the moment I met you. It will be yes for the rest of my life."

Tears stung the corners of my eyes and I pulled him to me for a long kiss. "I should have come up with a more special way to do this," I murmured as I reached into my pocket to pull out the ring. I'd been carrying the damn thing around ever since I'd talked to Dom and Logan. I'd kept hoping that having it with me would help me figure out when and where would be the perfect time to ask the question.

"I can't think of a better way than this," Eli whispered. "When it's just us...when we're facing so much uncertainty..."

I nodded and stood up, taking Eli with me so that we were both standing. My fingers shook as I opened the box. Eli bit into his lower lip at the sight of the ring and when I dropped to my knee, he let out a small cry. When I took his hands in both of mine, he gripped them tightly and I could tell he was struggling to hold it together. I wasn't doing much better as the emotion became too overwhelming.

"Eli Galvez, my lover, my best friend, my heart…will you marry me?"

Eli had started nodding the second I'd said his name and as soon as I finished the sentence he let out a guttural, "Yes," and dropped to his knees in front of me. We both laughed as I worked to get the ring on his finger and then he was wrapping his arms around my neck. I felt his tears against my skin and I had no doubt he could feel mine. He pulled back enough to kiss me and then we were wiping at each other's tears.

"I…I got you a ring too. I was going to ask you on Christmas day," he sputtered as he played with my fingers.

"Put it on me tonight when we go to bed," I said softly and I leaned down to kiss him again.

Eli nodded and then he was clinging to me again. "I love you, Mav," was whispered into my ear.

"I love you, Eli." We held on to each other for several long seconds before I climbed to my feet and pulled Eli up with me. "By the way, I promised Sylvie she could be the flower girl."

Eli laughed and said, "You talked to Sylvie about this?"

"Baby, I talked to practically your whole damn family."

That silenced him. He shook his head in disbelief. "I guess you really do love me," he finally said with a smile and then he was kissing me again.

"Damn right I do," I murmured against his mouth. When we separated again, Eli admired his ring and then pressed his hand to my chest. It looked so fucking perfect on him that I wondered what the hell I'd been thinking waiting so long.

"I'm going to go check on Caleb," Eli said.

I nodded and then watched him head for the hallway that led to the lower level guest room. I dropped back down in the chair and pulled out my phone, hoping there'd be a text from Jace. I had no idea when he was set to arrive and he hadn't answered when I'd tried calling him just before Eli had gotten home. At this point all I could do was wait…and hope like hell Jace had some answers as to how we could start putting the young man in the other room back together.

Chapter 10

HAWKE

I HELD THE DOOR OPEN AS A VERY TIRED LOOKING SETH MADE HIS way up the walkway, a little boy in his arms. Tristan was right behind him holding a little girl's hand and Memphis and Brennan brought up the rear.

"Hi," Seth said quietly.

"Hey," I said softly and I put my hand on his shoulder. "Living room," I directed.

Tristan smiled at me as he went by and I didn't miss how the little girl pressed closer to him as they passed me.

Memphis and Brennan each hugged me before entering the house. I saw Zane getting out of his car across the street and sent him a wave. I'd gotten the details of what had happened at the hospital when Memphis had called to see if they could bring the kids over to get some rest. Seth wasn't ready to be by himself with them after the events of the day and Ronan had stayed behind at the hospital to be with the older girl.

Once I reached the living room, I saw that Tate had already gotten the kids some juice boxes and he'd put some snacks on the table. Both Seth and Tristan were sitting on the couch, the kids in their laps.

Tate and Matty were sitting in one of the oversized chairs. We'd explained to Matty that the children that were coming over might be a little nervous so he was watching them with curiosity, but he stayed on Tate's lap. Brennan was sitting in the opposite chair and Memphis was sitting on the arm rest. I went and sat down next to Seth and kept my voice low when I said, "The girl?"

"She's okay. The doctors sedated her after..." Seth's voice dropped off as he glanced down at the little boy in his arms and I nodded in understanding. He didn't want the child to know his sister had been attacked.

"Jamie, this is my friend Hawke," Seth said as he turned Jamie so he could see me.

Jamie was sucking his thumb. His eyes met mine, but he didn't say anything.

"And that," – Seth pointed to Tate and Matty – "is Tate and that's Matty."

"Hi," Matty said with a small wave. I saw Jamie's eyes shift to Matty and interestingly enough, they stayed on him.

"Have they spoken at all?" I asked.

Seth shook his head. "Nicole was signing at the hospital, but she was doing it so fast and I'm still learning so I couldn't tell what she was saying. She stopped after the incident."

I glanced at the little girl who had her face pressed to Tristan's chest. Whatever had happened had clearly traumatized both kids.

"Papa, be right back, okay?" Matty said as he hopped off Tate's lap.

"Okay, buddy," I said and watched as Bullet and Storm both got up to follow my son towards his room. I didn't miss the fact that Jamie's eyes followed Matty from the room before he turned his head back against Seth's chest.

"What did Zane say?" I asked.

Seth seemed to understand what I was asking because he said, "He got approval from CPS for the kids to stay with us till they figure out what's going on. Gene, that's the uncle, is being held on assault charges. The wife, Alana, was questioned and released... Declan and Zane can't do much until Willow wakes up and makes a statement. Zane said he was going to file an emergency restraining order against both the aunt and the uncle."

I put my hand on Seth's back in an attempt to soothe him because I could tell he was beyond stressed. "Do you want to try to put the kids down for a bit? We've got a guest room or you can put them in our room or Matty's."

"That's probably a good idea," Seth murmured, but before we could get up, Matty reappeared followed by both dogs.

He walked up to me and asked, "Papa, can I talk to him?" as he motioned to Jamie.

"Yeah, buddy, but he's pretty scared, so he might not answer you, okay?"

Matty nodded. "Here," Matty said as he held out his beloved Spider-man doll to the little boy.

Jamie didn't respond in any way, but Matty wasn't deterred and when he moved to sit between me and Seth, I shifted so he'd have room. He plopped back against the couch cushion and began moving the doll's arms. To Jamie he explained, "He fights the bad guys. See, he's got these spider webs that shoot from his hands…" Matty pointed to the doll's wrists. "And he can climb up the sides of buildings and swing between them."

Jamie was resting his cheek on Seth's chest, but his eyes followed Matty's fingers as he pointed out things about the doll. "Here," Matty said again as he handed the doll to the little boy. Jamie didn't respond at first, but then he carefully pulled his thumb from his mouth and reached for the doll. Matty pitched forward so he was nearly face to face with Jamie. "He'll keep you safe," he whispered. "And you can keep him forever if you want," he added as Jamie clutched the doll against his body.

My chest swelled with pride and I glanced at Tate who had his hand over his mouth. I could see the emotion welling in his eyes as he watched our son.

"Are you sure you want to do that, buddy?" I said as I put my hand on Matty's shoulder. "He's your favorite, isn't he?"

"Yeah, but I don't need him anymore."

"You don't?"

Matty shook his head and leaned against me as his gaze shifted to Tate. "We're safe now, Papa. Daddy and me. So we don't need him anymore. Right Daddy?"

Tate swallowed hard and nodded before he managed to say, "Right."

Matty smiled brightly and then turned his attention back to Jamie. "Can he come play with me in my room?"

"Why don't you ask him?" I suggested.

Matty straightened and again got close to Jamie. "Wanna come play in my room?"

I didn't expect the little boy to actually respond, but he shocked all of us by nodding and then he put his hand out. Matty took it without hesitation and then got off the couch. Seth helped Jamie down and Matty began to lead him past Tristan, but Jamie tugged him to a stop and then handed the doll to Matty. We all watched in stunned silence as he tapped his sister's leg. He waited until she finally turned her head to look at him. His little fingers began flying in a rapid succession of movements that lasted only a few seconds. Nicole sat up a little bit and then looked around. Her eyes lifted to Tristan before they shifted to Matty. She signed something back and then Jamie held out his hand. She took it and climbed off Tristan's lap. Jamie reached for Matty's hand with his free one and I watched my son lead his new friends to his bedroom, Bullet and Storm on their heels.

"Wow," I heard Memphis say, but my eyes were on Seth because the second the kids were out of sight, his face fell and he covered his eyes with his hand. A harsh sob escaped his throat.

I put my arm around his shoulders. "Seth..."

"Sorry," he said in a choked voice and I could tell he was struggling to keep it together. But I suspected that after everything that had happened, that was the last thing he needed.

"Don't be sorry," I whispered to him and then I pulled him against my chest. He instantly let out an agonized cry and began sobbing. I barely noticed when Memphis, Tristan and Brennan got up and left the room, presumably to give Seth some privacy. Tate sat down on Seth's other side and put his hand on Seth's back in a gesture of comfort.

Several long minutes passed before Seth calmed down and when he finally straightened, Tate handed him some tissues. "Thanks," Seth murmured as he began wiping at his face. "I saw that gun this morning and thought it was real and she was pointing it at Ronan…" he began,shaking his head. "It all happened so fast and then she was on the ground and Ronan was doing CPR."

Seth paused as he sucked in a deep breath. "At the hospital I thought Ronan was going to be arrested and then the aunt and uncle show up and said they were taking the kids…"

Fresh tears began to fall and Tate got some more tissues. "They're safe now, Seth. Ronan too."

"I thought I could give them up if I had to…"

"You won't have to," I interjected. "Those fuckers aren't getting them back," I insisted, even though it wasn't something I was completely sure of.

Seth nodded and fell silent and I knew what he really needed was Ronan.

"Go call Ronan, Seth," I urged. "You can use our bedroom for privacy."

Seth looked at me and swiped at his eyes one last time. He began pulling out his phone when Matty appeared, Jamie and Nicole in tow. He stopped at Tate's side.

"Daddy, Jamie and Nicole are hungry. Jamie likes peanut butter and jelly sandwiches but the red jelly, not the purple. Nicole wants bananas on her sandwich."

All three of us were rendered momentarily speechless. Tate managed to recover first and he asked, "How do you know that's what they want, buddy?"

"They said so."

"They spoke to you?" Seth asked, trying to keep his voice calm and casual.

Matty nodded. "Nicole talks funny but Jamie said she said the word bananas."

Tate and I exchanged glances and then he was quickly getting up. "Okay, I'll make them right now."

As soon as Tate had moved out of the way, Seth moved over so he was closer to Matty. "Matty, can you do me a favor?"

Matty nodded.

"Can you ask Jamie and Nicole if they'll talk to me?"

"He can hear you, silly," Matty said as he shook his head. "But Nicole can't so he can ask her for you, okay?"

Seth smiled and nodded and then directed his question to Jamie. "Jamie, do you think you and Nicole can talk to me?"

Jamie glanced at his sister and then leaned forward to whisper something in Matty's ear.

"They can't," Matty announced. "They can't talk to grown-ups. Willow said so."

"Okay," Seth said as he looked at Jamie again. "But how come you didn't talk to the kids at the home?"

Matty obediently put his ear to Jamie's mouth and nodded. "Because they were mean to Nicole," he said solemnly. "Papa, they should get a talking to," Matty added as he looked at me.

"Yeah, buddy, they should," I agreed.

"Jamie, can you and Nicole tell Matty things and then maybe he can tell us?" Seth asked the little boy.

Jamie turned to Nicole and signed something. She nodded and then Jamie was whispering in Matty's ear again.

"He says yes…but he's hungry."

Seth chuckled and then looked at me.

"Okay, let's move this to the kitchen," I suggested. Matty took Jamie's hand and Jamie took Nicole's and the little human chain filed past us and towards the kitchen.

Chapter 11

RONAN

As soon as the girl startled awake, I was ready and I grabbed her gently by the shoulders to hold her down when she tried to jerk upright. "It's okay, you're safe," I said as I maintained my grip on her. It took very little effort because she was still weak. Her shoulders felt bony beneath my hands and I instantly gentled my hold even further just to make sure I wouldn't inadvertently leave any bruises on her.

"Nicole! Jamie!" she cried out, though the words came out as a hoarse whisper.

"They're safe," I assured her. "They're with my husband and our friends."

She settled slightly, but her wary eyes were clouded with distrust. When I was sure she wouldn't try to get out of bed, I grabbed the cup of water from the side table and held the straw to her mouth. Instead of drinking, she took the entire cup from me and despite her weak muscles, she held it close to her body as she began drinking.

"Just a few sips at a time," I warned her. She shot me a dark look, but she removed the straw from her lips and waited several long moments before taking another sip.

"I need to see them," she said as her hand went to her bruised throat.

I pulled out my phone and sent a text to Seth. I turned the phone so she could see the message and then sent it. "It will probably take him about half an hour or so to get here with the traffic."

Willow nodded and then glanced out the window. "What time is it?" she asked as she took in the overcast sky.

"Four o' clock."

Her hand went back to her throat. "Uncle Gene…is he…"

"He's in jail," I said. "Your aunt isn't in custody, but she's been ordered by a judge to stay away from you and your brother and sister. You have a lawyer named Zane Devereaux who is now your advocate. That means he will work with the courts and CPS to do what's best for you, Jamie and Nicole."

"So I don't have to talk to you," she responded.

"No, you don't."

"Am I going to jail?" she asked and I saw some of her hardness dissolve.

"No, but you're still facing charges for what happened this morning. Since you're a minor, you'll likely get probation. Zane will find you a good criminal attorney and if he can't, I'll find you one."

Her suspicion was clear, but she didn't respond right away. "What…what happens now?" she finally asked and I was reminded of how young she truly was.

"That depends on you," I said truthfully.

"What do you mean?" she asked.

"If you keep trying to do this on your own, you or Jamie or Nicole are going to end up hurt or worse. You almost died today, Willow. And since your heart actually stopped beating, technically you did die."

Willow paled and then reached to touch the wound on her side, but stopped short when I put my hand over hers to stop her. She jerked her hand back and immediately moved as far away from me as she could.

Pain went through me, but not because she'd reacted to *me* that way. But because she'd reacted that way at all.

"Was it just you or did he go after your sister and brother too?" I asked.

Willow stifled a gasp and her eyes shot to mine.

"Based on the way he grabbed your sister out in the waiting room, I'm guessing it was all of you. But I'm also guessing you took the brunt of it...maybe you made yourself a target?"

Willow dropped her eyes, but to my surprise, she nodded. "He'd get mad at Nicole all the time...he and Alana didn't know sign language and didn't want to learn it. But it's not always easy for Nicole to use words..."

"What did your aunt do?" I asked.

She just shook her head. It was answer enough. The bitch had done absolutely nothing.

"They said you came up here because you believed your parents were still alive."

Willow let out a huff and her mouth pulled into a frown. "Their car collided with a semi...I saw what was left of the car."

"Then why did you come up here?"

"Our mother had an aunt up here that we were really close to before our parents..."

Her voice dropped off for a moment and she used the need to take a drink to cover her attempt to control her emotions.

"What happened?" I asked gently.

"A neighbor told us she'd died about a month after our parents had. Uncle Gene never told us that."

"Why wasn't she given custody of you?"

"She had some health issues so the judge said we had to go live with Gene and Alana. He didn't give a shit that our father hadn't spoken to Gene in years."

"Gene is your father's brother?"

Willow nodded.

"Willow," I said softly and I waited until she looked at me. "Did he ever touch you or Jamie or Nicole in an inappropriate way?"

"No," she responded and her eyes never left mine. "If I'd thought for even a second he was doing that to them, I would have killed him," she said vehemently.

"Why not just call the cops and tell them about the physical abuse?" I asked.

Her eyes fell again. "I did. When they showed up and saw the bruise on my face, they questioned him. But he convinced them my boyfriend had done it and that I was accusing him because we'd gotten into a fight about me seeing him," she responded. "I don't even have a boyfriend. After they left, he put a knife to Jamie's throat and told me if I ever opened my mouth again…we ran the next day."

"Did he say something to you before he attacked you today?"

Her hand went to her throat again. "He just told me to keep my mouth shut. I couldn't breathe…"

"You have asthma," I said.

She nodded. "I don't get attacks very often."

"The attack you had this morning was probably brought on by stress. You'll still need to carry an inhaler, though." When she didn't respond, I asked, "What happened when you realized your great-aunt was gone?"

"I'd taken some money from Alana's purse the night before we ran. I used it to get us a hotel room and some food, but it didn't last very long. I found an abandoned building when we were walking on the streets one day. There were some mattresses in one of the rooms near the back. I was able to steal some of the other stuff we needed and I begged for money whenever I could. I didn't like leaving Jamie and Nicole, but I didn't have a choice…I couldn't take them with me when I was begging…or stealing," she said dejectedly. "I came back a few weeks ago to find them gone…this homeless guy told me he saw the cops taking them."

I saw a tear slide down her face, but she angrily wiped it away. "It took me forever to find them…I had to go to the library to use the computer to look up all the group homes in the city. I was sure I'd never find them, but then I saw them playing in the backyard of that group home a few days ago. But there were too many grown-ups around."

"That gun nearly cost you your life, even if it was fake," I said, my heart clenching as I relived the moment I saw Willow's body flying backwards, blood spraying into the air.

"I stole it from a toy store a long time ago...guys used to try and mess with me while I was asking people for money."

"Did any of them-"

"No," she interrupted. "No," she repeated softly. "When I saw you guys coming out with Nicole and Jamie this morning, I knew if I didn't do something, I'd never see them again..."

More tears fell. "I promised them I'd always take care of them...that we were still a family."

Willow put the cup on the tray table in front of her and then turned on her side away from me and curled in on herself as much as the IV and her injury would allow. I got up and sat on the edge of the bed and was glad when she didn't seem afraid.

"You'll take care of them, right?" she whispered before turning back enough so she could look me in the eye. "Nicole is really smart and she takes good care of Jamie. And Jamie..." her voice cracked. "Jamie's really sweet and well-behaved. He won't give you any trouble...just don't let Gene and Alana get them back."

When she tried to roll on her side again, I gently held her shoulder so she couldn't. "What about you?"

"What?" she asked.

"What are you like?"

She shook her head in confusion.

"Because I've seen that you're incredibly brave and smart, this morning notwithstanding." Willow didn't respond, but her eyes looked haunted.

"Willow, I guess what I really want to know is, do you and Jamie and Nicole have room in your family for a couple more people and one well behaved dog?" At that, Willow looked at me in surprise. "Because family's something my husband and I have been sorely lacking until recently. And we've both learned that you can never have too much family."

"Your husband?" she asked. "You're...you're married to a man?"

"Not just any man. The most amazing man you'll ever meet," I said softly. "A man who took one look at your brother and sister and knew they were meant to be ours. A man who I know even now is hoping like hell you'll want to be ours too."

Willow tried to sit up and I immediately reached for the bed controller and raised the head for her so she'd be more comfortable. "Even...even after what I did this morning?"

"You were trying to protect your family," I said. "The way you went about it may not have been the smartest in the world, but my husband knows what it means to fight for the people you love. And if you say yes, he'll spend the rest of his life fighting for you." I fought back the rush of emotion that threatened to overtake me as I whispered, "We both will."

Before Willow could respond, the door to the room was sliding open and Nicole tore through it as soon as her eyes landed on her sister.

She cried out her sister's name and then was trying to scramble up on the bed. I grabbed her before she could inadvertently land on her sister's injury and lifted her up and deposited her on Willow's other side. Nicole threw her arms around Willow's neck and began crying.

Jamie was holding on to Seth's hand when they walked into the room and I saw that the little boy was also on the verge of tears. I suspected he was intimidated by the environment and seeing all the machines surrounding his sister. Willow held out her free hand and Jamie turned and put his arms up. Seth lifted him and then carried him over to the bed. Once they reached it, Jamie put his arms out for his sister and I made sure to protect her side when Seth set the boy down.

Jamie put his hand to Willow's ear and whispered something to her before he looked over his shoulder at Seth. Love for my husband bloomed in my chest as he smiled at the little boy and then searched out my hand. Willow's eyes settled on our joined hands and I felt my heart skip a beat with worry. What if she fought this? Fought us?

But my concerns were put to rest when she ran her hand over her brother's head and said, "Yeah, Jamie, you can talk to him now." Her eyes settled on me. "You can talk to both of them."

Chapter 12

MAV

I HAD THE DOOR OPEN AS SOON AS I SAW THE HEADLIGHTS FLASH across the window. The first words out of Jace's mouth when he crossed over the threshold were, "Where is he?" The worry in his voice was enough to answer the question that had been nagging me from the moment Jace had told me he was on his way.

"He's resting," I said and as Jace made a move to pass me, I grabbed his arm to stop him. "We need to talk before you see him," I said. Jace's hard eyes lifted to mine, but he nodded and followed me into the small den that was just off the entryway. Eli was actually using the space to study so there wasn't any furniture besides a desk, a chair and some bookshelves. But I wasn't in the mood to sit and from the agitation that was rolling off of Jace in waves, I knew he wasn't either.

"What happened?" Jace asked.

"I need to ask you the same thing," I said quietly.

"What do you mean?"

"Last summer after you got him out of the hospital, you were alone with him for nearly two days."

Jace stiffened and his already dark eyes went black with anger.

"Is that what you think of me, Mav?" he asked. "You think I'd take advantage of a traumatized seventeen-year-old kid?"

"I don't want to believe it, but whatever attachment he's formed with you apparently hasn't eased even a little since you left nearly six months ago."

"Fuck you, Mav," Jace snapped and then he was reaching for the door handle. But I slammed my hand against the door to keep it closed.

"The cops found him standing on a bridge that is apparently some kind of fucking magnet for jumpers."

Jace's reaction was similar to what mine had been at the police station.

Utter disbelief.

"Now tell me what the fuck is going on between you two," I demanded. "Because we haven't been able to get more than a few words out of him at a time and today he's suddenly demanding to talk to you and only you."

"Nothing fucking happened, Mav!" Jace bit out. "Yeah, the kid's got some kind of hero worship thing going on because I got him out of that hospital, but that's it. I thought the sooner I left, the sooner his life would start to go back to normal again…even though I guess it never really was normal with what that fucker was doing to him."

"There has to be more than that!" I said in frustration.

"There isn't! Think about it, Mav. He watched his brother die at his father's own hand after being victimized by the man for most of his life. His mother was gone; Eli was gone…he had no one! So yeah, he latched on to me! He would have done it with anyone, though."

"So you don't have feelings for him?"

Jace opened his mouth to answer, but then snapped it shut.

"Jesus, Jace," I muttered.

"Nothing happened, Mav," he bit out. "Yeah, I felt sorry for him and I wanted to help him, but that was it. I never touched him…not the way you're thinking."

"What *did* you do?"

Jace turned away from me and began pacing and I was reminded of Caleb's behavior earlier in the day. "I held him," Jace finally said. "But that's it." He stopped and looked at me. "You should have seen him, Mav. He couldn't fucking sleep. He couldn't stop shaking. He kept whispering how cold he felt. So yeah, I held him while he slept. I comforted him when he needed it. But that's it."

The normally cool and detached Jace's voice was full of emotion so I knew that wasn't 'just it.' But I did believe that Jace was telling the truth about not doing anything inappropriate with Caleb physically.

"I did what I was supposed to do and got him back here," Jace murmured. "And I left as soon as I knew he was safe."

I didn't respond because it actually seemed like Jace was trying to convince himself rather than me that he'd done the right thing by Caleb.

"Have you talked to him since then?"

Jace shook his head. "He wanted my number, but I didn't give it to him…I knew he was getting too attached to me."

"We need to know if he was really considering hurting himself today, Jace," I finally said. "Eli and I want to bring him here to live with us so I can keep an eye on him, but we need to know what we're dealing with. He's refusing any kind of therapy and he's skipped so much school that he'll probably have to be held back a year. And with his father's trial coming up…"

Jace nodded. "I'll talk to him."

I nodded and opened the door and led Jace to Caleb's room. Caleb was lying on the bed and Eli was sitting on the small armchair we'd put in the room to serve as a place for guests to put their luggage. Baby was lying on the bed next to Caleb.

"Caleb, Jace is here," I said softly and I saw Caleb slowly turn his head to look over his shoulder at us. Tears flooded his eyes as he sat up and then he was climbing unsteadily to his feet. He really did look different from the young man we'd met the previous summer. His hair had gotten long and messy and he'd lost a lot of weight. Dark circles under his eyes overshadowed his gaunt face. God, how had we all missed how quickly the young man had spiraled downward? Why had we been content to believe he'd get better on his own?

"Jace?" Caleb whispered and then a harsh sob tore free of his throat and he walked into Jace's embrace.

Eli came to me and I took his hand and led him from the room, shutting the door behind us so Jace and Caleb could have some privacy. I knew Jace wouldn't take advantage of Caleb...I wasn't proud of the fact that I'd mentally gone there even for a little while, but Jace's behavior in the den had convinced me how much he cared about the young man.

I led Eli to the living room and we sat down on the couch and just held on to each other for a while. An hour passed without a peep from Caleb's room so Eli and I kept ourselves busy wrapping the many presents we'd ended up ordering online for Christmas. Between his family and mine, we hadn't even gotten halfway through the pile when we heard Caleb's door open.

Jace led Caleb into the living room and sat down with him on the couch. Their hands were intertwined and it looked like Caleb was holding on to Jace so hard that his fingers had actually gone bloodless.

The scene was eerily reminiscent of the day we'd met up with Caleb and Jace at the motel in the mountains of West Virginia. Caleb looked a little more relaxed despite the way he was clinging to Jace.

"I didn't go to the bridge to hurt myself," Caleb murmured. His eyes searched out Eli's. "I swear."

Eli nodded.

"This kid at school has a brother who works at a liquor store near the bridge. He sells to underage kids. After I paid him the fifty bucks he charges plus the cost of the alcohol, I didn't have any money left for a cab to get back home so I just started walking."

"The police officer who picked you up said you seemed to hesitate when he ordered you to step away from the side."

Caleb swallowed hard and glanced at Jace. "I wasn't thinking about jumping...I was thinking about when I was a kid and me and my mom and Nick would rent one of those paddle boats on a nice day and paddle around Lake Union. For the first time in a really long time, things in my head didn't seem so loud and I just wanted to hang on to that for as long as I could."

"Caleb," Eli whispered. "Please tell us how we can help you." I tightened my hand on Eli's because I could hear the raw pain and desperation in his voice.

"I don't know," Caleb whispered hoarsely. "I feel like I'm trapped in the dark and every once in a while, there's a flash of light, but all I see is Nick…and Dad. I hate him so much, Eli…but I miss him too. It's so…fucked up," Caleb said dejectedly.

Eli got up and moved to the couch to sit on Caleb's other side. "It's not, Caleb," he said softly. He was careful not to touch his brother. "I hate him for what he did to me…to us, but I still miss the fun stuff we did together…like going to baseball games or the movies or when he told me I could call him 'Dad.' I couldn't make sense of how I could still love someone who did those things to me." Eli finally reached up to gently push Caleb's hair off his face. "But talking to someone helped me make sense of those feelings."

Caleb nodded and wiped at the tears that had started to fall from his eyes. "Okay, I'll try…but I don't want anyone else there."

Eli nodded. "Okay," he agreed. "Mav and I were talking and we were thinking you might want to come stay with us for a while."

Caleb's eyes shifted briefly to me and then Jace. Caleb nodded again, but didn't say anything else.

"Caleb and I were talking about the wedding this weekend," Jace said. I knew he was talking about Hawke and Tate's wedding which was scheduled to take place at Seth and Ronan's house on Whidbey Island. "He wasn't sure he wanted to be around all those people so I was thinking he and I could explore the city a bit… maybe he can show me around."

I'd been torn about what we were going to do in terms of the wedding because I knew it wouldn't be a good environment for Caleb. He clearly wasn't in any shape to interact with both of our extended families. I'd already been planning to stay home with Caleb, but Jace was providing something I knew Caleb needed.

Peace.

Even if it was only for a day. And for whatever reason, being around Jace seemed to bring him peace like nothing else had.

"I think that's a good idea," I said. Caleb's eyes actually widened and I saw a sliver of hope in them and I knew I'd made the right choice. I'd told Eli about what Jace had said to me in the den and I knew he agreed with me that Jace wouldn't take advantage of Caleb. "Can I convince you to stay here at the house with us?" I asked. "The couch pulls out."

Jace nodded. "I'd appreciate that."

I suspected that between Caleb's exhaustion and Jace's comments that he'd held Caleb the previous summer at the motel so the young man could sleep, that Jace wouldn't be spending any time on the couch, but I wasn't about to tell the seventeen-year-old he could sleep with the man he was infatuated with. I was putting my faith in Jace that he wouldn't let things go any further than sleeping.

"Eli and I were planning on decorating our tree tonight," I said as I motioned to the Christmas tree Eli and I had finally managed to pick out a few days earlier. "You guys up for helping?" I asked.

Caleb sucked in a deep breath and I saw his grip on Jace finally ease. He looked at Eli and said, "I'd like that."

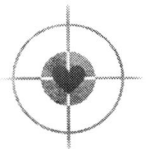

Chapter 13

MACE

"You thinking you want this someday?" I asked Memphis as I watched my men helping Tristan and Brennan string up the last of the lights across the ceiling in the glass sun room. The room had already been cleared out and set up with dozens of chairs and decorated with a mix of red and white flowers. The wedding arch was a simple combination of the same flowers, a few sprays of garland and pine cones and bright white lights. Jonas had mentioned to Hawke that hanging clear Christmas lights from the ceiling would make for a pretty scene as darkness fell. Hawke had readily agreed and despite it being the day before Christmas eve, my men had joined Tristan and Brennan in the search for lights at the local big box store while Memphis and I had stayed behind to let the caterers start setting up the tables for the reception that would happen after the ceremony the following day.

"Someday," Memphis said, but when I glanced at him, I saw a big smile on his face as his eyes lingered on Tristan and Brennan who were laughing about something. When he caught me looking at him, he chuckled and said, "Okay, yeah."

I laughed and took a sip from my bottle of water before setting it on a side table.

"What about you?" Memphis asked.

I nodded. "Definitely." I felt my insides draw up tight when Cole shot me a quick smile and I wondered if that feeling would ever go away. I sure as hell hoped not.

"We've talked about doing a ceremony," I admitted. "But nothing that would be legal," I added as I glanced at Memphis. "I'm not choosing one of them over the other for the sake of a piece of paper."

Memphis nodded in understanding. "Brennan and Tristan's uncles haven't legally married even after almost nine years together. But they share the same name, they have two beautiful daughters... none of that shit is because of a piece of paper." Memphis took a long draw on his beer before saying, "In their eyes and in the eyes of the people who love them most, they're as committed to each other as any married couple, gay or straight." We both fell silent for a moment, each lost in thought.

"Mace..."

I looked over at Memphis. "Yeah?"

"Thank you," the man said softly as he glanced at both his lovers. His eyes shifted back to me. "That day in New York...you made me see that something like this was possible. I'm...I'm not sure if I would have taken the risk if you hadn't."

My thoughts drifted back to the day Memphis had sought me out to ask me about my relationship with Jonas and Cole. Never in a million years had I expected that to be the topic of conversation when he'd asked me to meet him for coffee. But as I watched both of his young men sending him long, loving looks, I said, "You would have gotten there, Memphis." I nodded towards Brennan and Tristan. "No way in hell they would have let you get away."

Memphis smiled and I swore I saw a blush creeping up his throat. I laughed and decided to spare the man any additional embarrassment. "So Ronan and Seth are still attending tomorrow?" I asked. Memphis had given us the details about the three kids Ronan and Seth were taking in when he and Brennan had picked us up at the airport this morning.

"Yeah...they wanted to spend the night at their new house so the kids don't have to try to adjust to a new environment even for a night."

"So the girl is out of the hospital?"

"She got released a couple days ago. She has to take it easy for a couple of weeks, but I guess they're bringing all three kids to the wedding. Tristan and the younger girl have a bond so we'll sit with them during the ceremony since Seth and Ronan are the best men and if the kids get too overwhelmed, we'll deal with it. It sounds like they're adjusting pretty well now that Willow is out of the hospital."

"Ronan Grisham, husband and now father," I said with a smile. "Who would have guessed it?"

"First Hawke, now Ronan...you know what that means, right?" Memphis asked. "You're next."

"Next what?" Jonas asked as he came up to me and reached for my water. He dropped down onto my lap and wrapped his arm around my shoulders.

"Memphis seems to think it's our turn to do the father thing since Ronan and Hawke are both down for the count."

My heart swelled at the sight of the smile that spread across Jonas's mouth. Starting a family was something we'd talked a lot about, but in theory. Jonas ran his fingers through my hair. "Memphis is a very smart man," he said with a grin.

"Amen," Memphis responded before taking a drink from his beer.

"But I think it's going to be a close call," Jonas said casually.

"What do you mean?" I asked as I settled my hand on Jonas's thigh. I heard him suck in a sharp breath and he shot me a heated look.

"I think Memphis may have his hands full tonight and probably not in the way he's hoping," he said.

Memphis choked on his beer and swiped at his chin. "What do you mean?"

"I may or may not have heard a little bit of a conspiracy building. The name 'Nicole' was mentioned a few times."

"Shit," Memphis muttered, but I didn't miss the hint of wonder in his voice.

"And you," - Jonas continued to play with my hair as he spoke - "are not getting any younger and I really wouldn't mind having a little boy or little girl with dark eyes and dirty blond hair."

After I managed to get past the visual of sharing a son or daughter with Jonas and Cole, I said, "I'm partial to blue eyes." I glanced at Cole and said, "And black or brown hair works just fine for me." I lifted my mouth to Jonas's ear so only he could hear me. "I guess I'll just have to show you tonight how much staying power I still have."

Jonas blushed prettily and then his mouth was closing over mine. It wasn't until Memphis coughed that we both remembered his presence and Jonas tore his mouth from mine. We were both breathing hard and I glanced up to see Cole watching us with open hunger.

"I think that's our cue," Memphis said with a chuckle and then he was getting up. I watched him walk over to Brennan and Tristan and then he said something to both men that had them going from laughing and smiling to hungry and needy inside of a split second. I didn't even bother watching the trio anymore because I knew they'd be heading up to their room as quickly as I planned to get Cole and Jonas up to ours. "You about done here?" I asked Jonas as I let my finger trail up his inner thigh.

Jonas nodded and then his mouth was on mine again. "We can finish in the morning," he whispered against my mouth. By the time I got us both to our feet, Cole was at our sides and his mouth sealed over mine without even speaking a single word. Then he was kissing Jonas and I moved to stand behind Cole so I could skim my hands down his back and over his jean clad ass.

"You wanna take both of us tonight, baby?" I whispered into Cole's ear.

Cole tore his mouth from Jonas's and whispered a harsh, "Yes."

"You'll be sore tomorrow," I warned him as I nipped at the spot just behind his ear and then soothed it with my tongue.

"I better be," he growled and then he turned to face me. His kiss was violently needy and I gave his demanding tongue everything and then some. We turned our lust on Jonas and then we were hurrying up to our room. I had Cole flat on his back on the bed before Jonas even managed to close the door. I heard Jonas shuffling around in our luggage for the lube and I didn't miss the little grunts that spilled from his lips as he watched me and Cole together. There were days that watching us was all Jonas wanted to do and that never failed to turn Cole and me on even more.

Cole's hands gripped my ass as he began grinding our shafts together and I knew that despite the preparation it would take to make it safe for Cole to take us both at the same time, it would be a deliciously rough encounter. I lifted off Cole long enough to straighten so I could take my shirt off and he immediately followed me so that he was sitting on the edge of the bed. My shirt hadn't even cleared my shoulders when his teeth closed over one of my nipple rings and tugged hard.

"Fuck," I bit out and I grabbed his head to urge him on. By the time Jonas reached my side, he was already naked and he immediately dropped to his knees and began working my pants loose. I took over the task for him so he could focus on Cole's clothes. Cole had just gotten his shirt off while Jonas was working his pants loose when I snagged Cole's hair and forced his head back. He groaned at the show of dominance. I nipped at his jawline and said, "We're going to fill that tight little hole of yours so good."

"Yes," Cole hissed and then his mouth was seeking out mine. But I refused to kiss him and instead manhandled his head until he was kissing Jonas. I knew both my men loved it when I took over just as I loved it when they did the same to me.

I watched them kiss and then I urged Cole's mouth to my cock. He swallowed me down in one try and I could see that Jonas had done the same to him. I leaned over Cole's back as I began fucking his mouth and let my hand trail down his skin until I could grip his ass cheeks and spread them. Cole groaned around my dick and I cursed at the sensation it left behind. I got my finger wet and searched out Cole's hole and began to toy with him as he deep throated me. But I knew I was too close to take much more, so I grabbed Cole by the hair again and dragged him off my dick. His eyes were bright with lust and I could taste my own essence when I kissed him. I released Cole long enough to pull Jonas off Cole's dick and I kissed him long and deep.

"Lie down on your back," I said to Jonas and he immediately complied. His dick was full and flushed a deep red. I turned Cole around and forced him down on the bed so he was hovering over Jonas's dick, his ass in the air. I leaned over Cole and let my dick slide through his crease as I said, "Don't make him come. If he does, I'm going to fuck you slow and deep until you get him hard again. Do you understand?"

Cole moaned and nodded and then his mouth was sucking Jonas deep. I watched Jonas grab Cole's head to try and control his movements, but Cole grabbed both his hands and pinned them to the bed. I searched out the lube Jonas had put down on the bed and began prepping Cole even as I enjoyed the sight of them going at each other.

"Cole, please," Jonas begged as he writhed against Cole's mouth.

I had no doubt Cole would have loved to give Jonas what he wanted, but I reminded him what was to come when I plunged a well lubed finger into his ass in one swift move. He let out a harsh cry and pushed back against my hand. I fucked his ass a few times and then pulled my finger free to put more lube on it. I slid the finger back inside of him, but avoided his prostate. His hole clenched around my digit in anticipation so I pulled out and added a second finger.

"Fuck," Cole growled and he stopped sucking on Jonas's dick. Sweat was starting to break out all over his body and I let my free hand slide up and down his back as I continued to loosen him.

"You ready for three, baby?" I asked.

Cole only managed a nod. At some point he'd released Jonas's wrists and Jonas was petting him gently as Cole rested his head on Jonas's abdomen. I added a third finger and twisted my wrist. Cole gasped and then he buried his face against Jonas. I waited until Cole's body began to relax again with every thrust I gave him and as soon as he began pumping his ass on my fingers, I knew we were almost there.

"Do you want four, Cole?"

It was the moment Cole needed to decide if he wanted to continue. It wasn't the first time we'd done double penetration, but it wasn't something we did often either. This would, in fact, only be Cole's second time having Jonas and me inside of him at the same time.

"Four," Cole sputtered. "Please, Mace, I want it!"

I leaned over Cole's back and whispered his name. When he turned his head, I seized his mouth in a bruising kiss. "You are so fucking beautiful like this, Cole."

Cole nodded and I saw him swallow hard. And I knew that it wasn't because I had three fingers jammed up his ass either. No, he was struggling with the same emotions Jonas and I were. No matter how rough we were when we came together, it always ended up like this...where it was still making love even when others might call it fucking. I paused long enough to kiss Jonas and then I leaned back to focus on what I was doing.

I added more lube to my fingers and then carefully began working all four of them inside of Cole. I took my time and allowed his body to suck me in rather than forcing it to accept the intrusion. I nodded at Jonas who reached for the lube and began slicking up his cock. Cole had managed to lock his elbows to give Jonas room to prepare himself and I didn't miss the fact that Jonas added some lube to Cole's dick and began jacking him off since he'd started to soften when I'd pushed the third finger into him.

It took several minutes before I was satisfied Cole's hole was loose enough. "Move forward," I urged Cole softly. I carefully removed my fingers as Cole settled himself over Jonas and as he began to lower his ass, I took Jonas's slick cock in hand and pressed it inside of Cole. I was pleased to see Jonas's shaft easily slide into Cole's body. Jonas gasped and pressed his fingers into Cole's thighs. Cole began riding Jonas as I prepped my own dick, but the sight of Jonas thrusting up into Cole proved to be too much for me and I climbed onto the bed behind Cole. I didn't speak as I used my weight to urge Cole to bend at the waist until he was lying flush against Jonas. Jonas's hands came up to close around Cole's back and he stopped moving.

"Cole?" I asked softly and he nodded.

"Give it to me, Mace. I need more."

I kissed the back of his neck and then I leaned back enough and began to press my dick against his opening. To say it was tight was an understatement. And the feel of Jonas's shaft nestled against my crown made my whole body feel like it was on the verge of exploding.

Once I was sure the head was past Cole's outer muscles, I used my hands to steady Cole's hips so he wouldn't inadvertently push back against me and force too much of me inside of him too quickly.

"Shit," Cole said harshly and then his mouth was on Jonas's.

Jonas kept his lower half perfectly still even as his mouth and hands worshipped Cole. I let out a muffled curse when Cole's inner muscles finally gave way and my crown completely disappeared inside of him. The sheer heat and pressure was exquisite, but I managed to maintain control of myself as I slid my dick into Cole inch by gloriously slow inch. The feel of my dick sliding against Jonas's was mind blowing and when my eyes met his over Cole's shoulder, I could see he was struggling to keep it together.

It took several minutes to safely work myself completely into Cole's body and then I just held there for a few moments to relish in the sensation of Cole's smooth walls gripping me so tight along with the heat wafting off Jonas's cock.

I nodded to Jonas and saw his hand slip between his and Cole's bodies. He began stroking Cole's dick, but it wasn't until Cole began moving just a little bit that I knew he was ready and I slowly pulled back before carefully sliding forward again.

Cole let out a harsh shout, but he pushed back against me as I slid in until I was balls deep inside of him. I repeated the move over and over again until it was Cole who was setting the pace.

"More," Cole muttered as he looked over his shoulder at me.

It was then that Jonas began moving and whatever control Cole had disappeared as Jonas and I took over his pleasure. Cole clung to Jonas as we ramped up the pace, the lube making our movements easier. Jonas didn't have as much free rein to move as I did, but he still managed full, deep thrusts that had me seeing stars, so I knew Cole had to be on a whole other plane of awareness. Within minutes, we were all groaning and Cole's body was so slick with sweat that I had to dig my fingers into his sides to maintain my hold on him. My hair clung to my face as I drove into Cole, but I didn't want to stop for even a second to push it off. Cole was writhing between us as Jonas began jerking him more frantically and I could tell he was close.

I leaned my body over Cole's back, bracing myself with my hands so Jonas wasn't carrying our combined weight. "So fucking hot, Cole," I muttered against his ear as I began ruthlessly fucking into him. I bit into his shoulder before saying, "Come for us, baby. Make us feel that tight ass trying to keep us both inside of you."

Cole's breath was coming in short bursts as he began bucking beneath me, trying to get us both deeper. "So close," he said with a guttural moan.

I nodded to Jonas. A moment later he thrust into Cole hard.

"Yes!" Cole shouted and Jonas did it again. Every time Jonas pushed in, I pulled out. The rest of the words that fell from Cole's mouth was just gibberish because his orgasm took over and his inner muscles clamped down on me and Jonas so hard that we both stopped moving for fear we'd inadvertently hurt Cole if we kept up our brutal thrusts. My own release threatened to knock me on my ass with its intensity and I pressed my mouth against the back of Cole's neck to stifle my scream of pleasure. Liquid heat bathed my cock and I knew the release wasn't all mine because I heard Jonas cry out Cole's name even as his hands closed around my wrists. Wave after wave of pleasure rolled through all of us and my body shook violently as the climax rose and crested over and over again. By the time the pleasure began to fade, my entire body pinned Cole flat against Jonas and my cock was still trying to empty itself inside of Cole even though it had nothing left to give.

We were all in a daze as we lay there trying to catch our breath.

"Cole," I whispered against Cole's ear because he was just a little too quiet.

"So worth it," he said softly as he turned his head.

"What is?" I asked as I placed soft kisses on his brow.

"Not being able to walk tomorrow."

I chuckled and then leaned past him to kiss Jonas. "Love you both so much," I murmured. Jonas told me he loved me, but I barely understood Cole's words because his eyes had drifted shut and I knew he'd be out within a minute or two. I reluctantly withdrew from him which he surprisingly barely noticed and then I gently worked Jonas's cock free. I went to the bathroom to get some washcloths and returned to the bed and cleaned both my men off. Jonas was cradling Cole against his chest and murmuring softly to him. I tossed the washcloths on the nightstand and then grabbed the edge of the comforter. I lay down at Cole's back and pulled the comforter across the three of us as best I could.

Jonas linked his fingers with mine where they were resting on Cole's side. "Did you mean it?" he whispered.

"Mean what?" I asked.

"A kid with blue eyes...do you really want that?" he asked.

My thoughts drifted to where they always did whenever kids were mentioned. But the memory of my son no longer paralyzed me like it used to. Instead, there was a feeling of warmth and I remembered the years I'd had with him and not the ones I'd lost. The idea of sharing that kind of joy with my men was something I couldn't even put words to.

"I meant it," I said. "Just like I meant it when I told Memphis I wanted the whole wedding thing."

Jonas smiled and I saw his eyes go bright with unshed tears. He pulled my hand up to his mouth and kissed the knuckles. "I want that too."

"Me too," Cole said softly between us and I smiled. I leaned down to kiss his cheek.

"Sleep, baby," I said softly. "We'll talk about it tomorrow." I looked at Jonas and said, "All of it."

Jonas nodded and then he snuggled closer to Cole and shut his eyes. And a few minutes later as their breathing evened out, I closed my eyes and dreamed of blue eyed, dark haired sons and daughters.

Chapter 14

RONAN

"Merry Christmas, Ronan," I heard Seth whisper into my ear. He was curled at my back and I could feel his lips press against my shoulder.

"It's only Christmas eve," I reminded him as I turned over to face him.

His fingers came up to play with my hair. "Every day has felt like Christmas," he said softly.

I knew exactly what he meant. It had only been a few days since our lives had been irrevocably changed and we were still riding the high of the realization that we were fathers and that we finally had the family we'd always dreamed of.

Neither of us were foolish enough to believe things would be easy with suddenly taking in three very traumatized kids, but there'd been a moment last night where we'd both just known that things would be okay. It hadn't been some dramatic turn of events where all three kids were declaring their love for us and calling us *Dad* or anything…no, it had been much subtler than that.

Seth and I had made dinner and had set the table like we had all the previous nights, but instead of Willow and the younger kids appearing and taking their plates and going back to the single bedroom they'd insisted on sharing, they'd actually sat down at the table with us. No, there hadn't been a lot of conversation or anything, but when we'd finished, they'd helped us clear the table and they'd each said their thank yous to us. When Seth had suggested we watch a movie together, the trio had "spoken" to one another using sign language and then Willow had said yes. We'd ended up watching a family-friendly cartoon movie with the subtitles turned on together in the den. Jamie had sat next to Seth and eventually fallen asleep against him. And instead of picking any of the several pieces of furniture to sit on, Willow had sat down next to me with Nicole on her other side. Bullet had ended up draped over Nicole's lap.

And just like that with a shared meal and all of us piled onto one couch with bowls of popcorn between us, we'd become a family.

"It has," I said as I leaned in to kiss him. A glance at the clock showed we had a couple of hours before we needed to start getting ready to head to the island house for the wedding, but before I could even get up to lock the door so Seth and I could have some private time, I heard it swing open. We'd been locking the door at night when we made love, but afterwards we unlocked and left it partially open so we could hear the kids if they needed something. We'd also started wearing pajama bottoms which we'd both laughed about since *that* had been an adjustment in itself.

Seth and I both sat up to see Jamie standing in the doorway, Bullet by his side and his Spiderman doll dangling from his hand. We hadn't managed to get any of the kids' stuff from Alana and Gene because we needed to wait for the custody case to be finalized so I was glad Matty had given him the doll, because it had clearly become a safety blanket to him in a way that none of the new toys we'd bought him could.

The pending custody fight was still a glaring concern, but Zane and Declan had both assured us the kids were ours. Gene was being charged with assault and the incident when Willow had called the cops to seek help for Gene's abuse was being re-opened. And even if Alana hadn't actually abused the kids herself, the fact that she'd stood by and let it happen left her without a leg to stand on. Even if she claimed the man was abusing her as well, she was in no position to regain custody.

"Jamie, is everything okay?" Seth asked, but before he could get out of bed, Jamie was walking towards us.

He stopped by Seth's side of the bed. "Willow's snoring," he muttered drowsily.

"She is?" Seth said with a chuckle as he glanced at me.

We had enough bedrooms for all three kids, but so far they'd all been sharing the room we'd set aside for Nicole.

Jamie nodded and then he was trying to climb up on the bed. Seth lifted him up and we both watched in shock as he crawled between us. He dropped his head on Seth's pillow and clutched the doll to his chest and closed his eyes. Bullet jumped on the bed and pressed between us so he could curl himself over Jamie's legs.

Seth and I smiled at each other and then rearranged ourselves until we were all comfortable. Seth wrapped his arm around Jamie's waist and I settled my hand on his arm. We didn't speak again.

We didn't need to.

"How are you holding up?" I asked Hawke as I entered the guest bedroom where he was getting ready.

He was sitting on the bay window still dressed in his street clothes. His hands were pressed together and his elbows were resting on his knees. Matty's puppy, Storm, was lying at his feet, but as soon as she saw me she came loping over to greet me. I hadn't changed into my tux yet so I let her jump on me as I scratched her floppy ears.

"Good," he said, though his voice was shaky. "Is he here yet?"

I hid the smile at how nervous my friend sounded and said, "He got here a few minutes ago."

The whoosh of air that left Hawke's body was a surprise. Did the man even think for a second that Tate would get cold feet?

I knew the couple had decided to honor tradition and spend the evening before their wedding apart. Tate and Matty had gone to stay with Tate's mom and her family at a bed and breakfast a few miles away and Hawke had gone to dinner with Magnus, Zane and Connor before returning to his home to spend the night by himself with just Storm to keep him company.

I went to sit on the bed across from Hawke and said, "Hey, I'm sorry Seth and I haven't been there for you guys-"

"Are you fucking kidding me?" Hawke interrupted. He motioned around him. "All of this...the fact that we're even here today is because of you and Seth." He clutched his hands together again before saying, "If you hadn't brought him back to me..."

Hawke's voice dropped off, but I knew he was thinking about the day Seth and I had taken Matty and Tate to Hawke's house in Wyoming a month after they'd ended their tenuous relationship.

"How are the kids doing?" Hawke asked.

"Good," I said. "Better than expected, actually," and I couldn't help the grin that split my lips.

Before I could say anything else, I heard a quiet knock on the door. "I got it," I said to Hawke and then I went to answer it. Matty entered followed by Jamie and Leo. Matty was holding one of Jamie's hands and Leo was holding the other. Matty was wearing the tux that matched his fathers' so I grabbed Storm by the collar when she made a beeline for him and held her back.

"Hi, Papa," Matty said as he hurried to Hawke and he dropped Jamie's hand so he could wrap his arms around his father.

"Hi, buddy," Hawke said with a sigh and he scooped the little boy up and held him in what I knew had to be a pretty tight embrace.

"Papa, Daddy said to tell you something."

"Okay, what is it?" Hawke asked as he pulled back a little from Matty.

"He said to tell you he missed you last night..." Matty paused as he seemed to need a minute to try to remember the rest of the message. "Oh yeah, and he never wants to do it again."

"Do what again?" Hawke asked in confusion.

Matty seemed stricken and then he glanced over his shoulder at me and curled his finger to motion me over. I held onto Storm as I leaned down to Matty's level and he reached into the small pocket on his vest and pulled out a scrap of paper. I read the note and smiled as I realized Tate had suspected his son might have trouble remembering the whole message.

I put my mouth against Matty's ear and whispered the rest of the message. Matty nodded and then turned back to Hawke.

"He doesn't want to spend a night apart from you ever again," Matty said proudly. "And he'll see you soon."

I saw Hawke's eyes darken with emotion and he clutched his son to him. I used their intimate moment to crouch down next to Jamie and Leo.

"Are you doing okay, Jamie?" I asked.

He nodded.

"Matty and I are watching out for him," Leo declared. I was glad to see the little boy was still wearing his pants, but from the way he was scratching at the waistband, I had to wonder how long it would last.

"You are?" I asked.

Leo nodded enthusiastically. "He's gonna sit with me while Matty helps his daddies get married."

I smiled at that and couldn't stop myself from running my hand over Jamie's hair. The little boy hadn't been talking to me as much as he did Seth, but I knew it was just a matter of time. The fact that he didn't pull away from me was progress as far as I was concerned.

"Thank you for taking care of him, Leo," I said and I dropped my hand on the beaming boy's shoulder.

I heard a knock on the door and saw Magnus waiting in the entry way. The older man looked distinguished in his dark suit.

"Just came to see how things are going in here," he said as he walked into the room.

"Good, Pop-pop," Matty said. He gave Hawke a quick kiss on the cheek and whispered, "See you soon, Papa."

"Yeah, buddy," Hawke said, his voice sounding gravelly.

Matty ran up to his grandfather to give him a hug and then went back to Jamie and Leo and grabbed Jamie's hand.

"Matty," Hawke called and Matty turned around. When Hawke motioned him over, Matty eagerly ran to him and I watched as Hawke leaned down to whisper something in his ear. Matty listened attentively and then nodded.

"I'll tell him, Papa," he said softly and then he hugged Hawke again before he collected Jamie and Leo and left the room.

"I was hoping I could have a word with you," Magnus said to Hawke.

"Of course," Hawke replied.

"I'm going to take Storm to the study," I said as I straightened as best I could while still maintaining my hold on the dog's collar.

"Thanks, Ronan," Hawke said softly.

I left the room, closing the door behind me, and led the puppy down the stairs. Bullet was already in the office lying on the couch so as soon as I lifted the child safety gate, Storm bolted into the room to join the German Shepherd. But that lasted all of ten seconds because the young dog then noticed that Memphis's cat, Tink, was lounging on one of the arm chairs. Tink ignored the puppy's antics as she tried to get the cat's attention, but wasn't quite brave enough to actually risk irritating her.

I chuckled as I put the safety gate back in place and then headed towards the living room where the guests who'd already arrived had started to congregate. The weather had ended up cooperating and while it wasn't warm enough to have the ceremony outside, it was a sunny and surprisingly dry day so we'd left the front door open so people could come in on their own if the young woman we'd hired to take coats and direct guests was busy.

My guess was that more than half the guests had arrived, but my focus was on the two girls sitting in the far corner of the room near the fireplace. My plan had been to go check on Willow and Nicole, but I hesitated when I saw Cade and Rafe's eleven-year-old daughter, Rebecca Barretti and thirteen-year-old Hannah Devereaux talking to both girls. I stood back to watch and smiled when I saw Willow showing both girls how to sign something to Nicole.

"Ronan," I heard someone say and saw Dom Barretti heading

towards me, his husband right behind him. They were holding hands and Dom released Logan's hand only long enough to shake mine.

"Glad you could make it," I said.

"How are the grooms holding up?" Logan asked.

I chuckled and said, "I've only seen Hawke but let's just say he's very, very ready to do this."

Dom chuckled and glanced at his husband. "Been there, done that."

Logan smiled and leaned in to brush a kiss over Dom's lips. "You practically dragged me down the aisle."

Dom's look turned heated as he growled, "Can you blame me?"

I laughed and shook my head because I knew exactly what they were talking about.

"Dom, Logan!"

I turned to see Mav and Eli making their way towards us. Dom and Logan immediately wrapped their arms around their son and I shook Mav's hand. My eyes fell on the silver and brass ring on Mav's finger and I smiled. When I lifted my eyes to meet Mav's, he was smiling widely and nodded. I understood the silent message and I didn't need to look at Eli's hand to know that I'd see the beautiful white gold and black ring there.

I embraced Mav. "Congratulations," I whispered in his ear.

"Thank you," he murmured. "For everything."

When I pulled back, I saw that Dom and Logan were admiring Eli's ring so I quietly said, "Caleb?"

"He's okay," Mav said. "He's with Jace."

That surprised me, but before I could ask, Mav said, "I'll tell you all about it later."

I nodded.

"Ronan?"

At the sound of my name, I looked up to see two men walking towards us and I smiled. "You made it."

"Wouldn't miss it," the older of the two men said as he reached out his hand. Cash Malloy was in his late thirties and was built like a tank. With his dark hair and even darker eyes, the man always had a dangerous look to him and I rarely saw him smile even when he was in the company of the guy who was more than just his partner in my group. Sage Brighton was Cash's polar opposite with his reddish brown hair that nearly touched his shoulders and the perpetual smile on his face. I didn't know exactly when the two men had started up a personal relationship, but it had been going on from almost the moment they'd both joined my organization within a few months of one another and had been assigned to partner up on a case. Since then, they always worked cases together and since they were such an accomplished team, I'd never even considered splitting them up.

Sage leaned in to hug me and then he and Mav were chatting.

"Ronan, look who I found," I heard Memphis say and he pushed his way through the group of men. I smiled at the sight of Daisy practically being dragged behind him. My IT girl clearly looked like she'd rather be anywhere else.

I wrapped my arms around the young woman. "Thank you for coming," I said softly in her ear.

"Well, he" – she motioned to Memphis – "practically made it an order."

I chuckled because I had no doubt that was true. Daisy's comfort zone was located on the opposite side of a computer screen.

"You look beautiful," I murmured as I released her and studied the long floral print dress that hugged her curvy figure and floated softly around her legs. Her long brown hair was pulled into a loose ponytail that hung down well past her shoulders.

"He picked it out," she whispered as she once again motioned to Memphis.

I laughed and hugged her again. "I promise you can change as soon as the ceremony is over."

That earned me a chuckle. I began introducing her to the other men, but when we reached Sage and Cash, I saw her hesitate.

"So this is the infamous Daisy," Sage drawled as he reached for her hand and held it a lot longer than he needed to. I didn't miss the electricity that flared to life between the pair, but Daisy pulled her hand free as quickly as she could without seeming rude.

"Nice...nice to meet you," she stammered as she dropped her eyes.

I sent Sage a hard look, but he seemed clueless as his eyes stayed on Daisy. What the hell? Was he actually interested in her? My eyes shot to Cash, but to my surprise, he too was staring at the young woman.

"Daisy," Cash murmured softly as he held out his hand.

That was it. He didn't say anything else, but the way he said her name had me wondering what the hell I was missing.

Daisy shook Cash's hand and nodded, but she didn't speak and she struggled to maintain eye contact with him. When she spied Mav, she got the escape she clearly needed and she hurried to him. The pair had worked together early on when I'd hired Daisy so she seemed much more comfortable with him than she did with anyone else. But her behavior with Cash and Sage seemed odd.

"What the hell was that?" I asked the pair as they both continued to watch Daisy.

"What?" Sage finally asked as he looked at me. He smiled and said, "We've talked with her on the phone a few times. It was nice to put a face with the voice, that's all."

"She's just not what we expected, Ronan," Cash said quietly and then he was snagging Sage's arm. "We'll catch you later."

Memphis stepped to my side and I asked, "Do you know what that's all about?" as I motioned to where Daisy was still talking to Mav, but kept shifting her eyes to Sage and Cash as they passed her.

"Not sure," Memphis said. "But they've got a lot of calls between them."

"Sage and Cash?" I asked in confusion.

"Sage and Daisy...even when Sage and Cash aren't working a case."

"Keep an eye on it," I said softly.

"You know Sage is harmless...he'd never hurt her in a million years and he's a hundred percent committed to Cash," Memphis said.

"She's got no one, Memphis, and for all her abilities with a computer, she's not exactly a social butterfly. A guy like Sage could fuck with her head without even meaning to."

"I'll take care of it," Memphis assured me. "Shouldn't you be getting ready?" he asked me and I glanced at the clock on my phone.

"Yeah," I responded and then I searched out Willow and Nicole again. They were still talking to Hannah and Rebecca. Another search showed Jamie was with Leo and Mrs. Finney. He was showing the old woman the Spiderman doll Matty had given him. I had no doubt it would just be a matter of time before he was racing Mrs. Finney in her electric wheelchair like Leo and Matty often did. My only hope was that he'd do it with his clothes on.

"I'll catch you in a bit," I said to Memphis. "We need to talk to Magnus after the ceremony," I reminded him. My eyes automatically went to Dante as I spoke and I saw that he was chatting with one of the young men who was part of the catering staff.

"He's not going to like it," Memphis murmured.

"Which one?" I asked.

"Either."

I nodded at that. I had no idea why Magnus and Dante seemed to rub each other the wrong way, but I also didn't really give a shit because my primary concern was making sure the older man was safe when he returned to Texas next week to testify in a high-profile case. And while Dante wasn't the easiest guy to deal with in terms of personality, he had killer instincts and in a situation where there was no credible threat, that trait would come in handy. The bottom line was that I would do whatever it took to make sure Matty's grandfather came home to his grandson.

"I'm not giving either of them a choice," was all I said in response and then I went to find Seth so I could give my husband an update on how our kids were doing before we stood at our friends' sides to help them celebrate this next chapter in their lives.

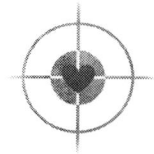

Chapter 15

HAWKE

WHAT THE HELL IS WRONG WITH ME?

My fingers wouldn't stop shaking as I tried to tie my bow tie.

"Here," I heard Magnus say as he stepped up next to me and gently pushed my fingers away from the silky material.

"I don't know why I'm so nervous," I admitted. "I know Tate wants to marry me…"

Magnus chuckled. "I think it's less about worrying he'll get cold feet and more about just wanting to get started on this new chapter in your lives."

I nodded my head, but stopped when Magnus said, "Hold still."

As soon as Ronan had left, I'd started getting dressed as I'd rambled on and on to Magnus about our plans for the following day as well as the one-night honeymoon we were planning before our actual honeymoon began.

After the reception tonight, we were planning to head back to our house with Matty so he could wake up Christmas morning in his own bed and we would have that moment where he realized Santa had come. Magnus would be joining us in the morning to open presents and then we'd be spending the afternoon with the entire extended family at Logan and Dom's house in the San Juan Islands.

Magnus had agreed to babysit Matty for us tomorrow night so Tate and I could spend a night together at a quaint Bed and Breakfast in Friday Harbor and then we were planning on leaving for our real honeymoon in a couple of days. The first half of the honeymoon would be spent with Matty in Disney World. We'd convinced Zane and Connor to let us take Leo with us so Matty could have his best friend with him. After a week at Disney World, we were going to take Matty and Leo home and Matty would spend ten days with Zane and Connor while Tate and I went to Santorini, Greece for the rest of our honeymoon.

"There," Magnus said as he turned me so I could examine his handiwork in the mirror. The bow tie looked perfect. I went back to the window seat and sat down so I could get my shoes on.

"Hawke," Magnus said quietly and I looked up to see him looking at me with all seriousness. It took me a moment to remember he'd wanted to talk to me about something when he'd come in.

I pulled my shoes on and then focused all my attention on him. The man actually looked nervous and I steeled myself for bad news. Had he decided against moving up here permanently, choosing instead to stay in Texas? That would fucking devastate Matty. Me and Tate too, since we'd grown close to the man in the months he'd been helping us get Matty through his chemotherapy treatments.

"I...I wanted to say thank you," Magnus began and I felt my heart constrict painfully. Shit, that sounded like the start of a kiss-off speech.

"For what?" I asked when he didn't continue on his own.

Magnus sat down on the bed. "For giving me my grandson back." His voice got rough as he whispered, "For letting me know Jenna..."

I remained quiet as Magnus tried to collect himself and didn't interrupt him or press him in any way. We hadn't ever talked much about his daughter and I could see that the pain of his loss still tormented him, despite how well he appeared to hide it around all of us.

"For letting me know Jenna wasn't coming home." Magnus paused and took a few deep breaths before he lifted his eyes to look at me. "You and Tate didn't have to welcome me into your family the way you did."

"Magnus," I began, but he held his hand up.

"I couldn't have asked for better parents for Matty. I know…I know I'm not that much older than you, but…" His voice dropped off again and he shook his head. "I know Tate's mom is walking him down the aisle. I'd…I'd be really honored if I could join you when you're walking down it."

Emotion clogged my throat and I couldn't speak so I was helpless to say anything and my silence clearly made Magnus uncomfortable.

"Not as your father or anything," he quickly clarified and he dropped his eyes again. "I mean-"

"Magnus" I cut in as I stood up. "I would love it," I whispered as tears stung my eyes. "Call yourself whatever you want…father, brother, friend," I began before I too was forced to pause to gather myself. "Just take that walk with me, okay?"

Magnus smiled and nodded. He stood and hugged me hard. No words were necessary as he stepped back and patted me on the arm. "You ready for this?" he asked, his voice lighter than it had been.

"I've never been more ready for anything in my life," I responded and it was true. In that moment all I really wanted to do was hunt down Tate and drag him in front of the minister so I could bind him to me forever, ceremony and guests be damned.

Luckily, I didn't have to curb the impulse for too long because there was a knock at the door a moment later and then Mav was sticking his head into the room and saying, "It's time."

❖

I DIDN'T ACTUALLY SEE ANY OF THE FACES OF THE MEN AND WOMEN

seated in the nearly dozens and dozens of elegant guest chairs that had been set up in the sun room. All I saw were the hundreds and hundreds of sparkling lights dancing above our heads as Magnus and I entered and waited for Seth and Ronan to get to the arch where the minister was waiting. Seth and Ronan held hands all the way down the aisle and I saw them kiss softly before splitting up to each go to one side of the arch which was sitting on a small, raised platform. Darkness was just starting to fall outside, casting a hauntingly beautiful shade of gray-blue over the water and mountains that were serving as the backdrop. The room was quiet except for the sound of Tristan playing Pachelbel's *Canon*, the wedding music Tate and I had chosen for our walk down the aisle. Ronan and Seth had had the piano moved from where it normally sat in the living room to the sun room especially for the occasion.

I hadn't yet seen Tate, but I knew he'd enter as soon as I reached the minister. I dropped down to give Matty a quick hug. "You okay, buddy?" I asked.

Matty nodded and patted his jacket pocket. "I've got them, Papa," he whispered. We'd learned our lesson at Ronan and Seth's wedding that putting the rings in Matty's pants pocket hadn't been the best idea.

"Okay, go do your thing. We'll be right behind you, okay?"

Matty nodded and then he was giving Magnus a hug. "Love you, Pop-pop."

"Love you too," Magnus whispered. "Go get 'em," he said with a wink.

Matty began his walk down the aisle and Magnus and I waited several beats before we followed. But after just a few steps, there was a loud crash from somewhere inside of the house and we heard someone shouting. Everyone froze for a moment and then I heard what sounded like metal hitting the floor. The music stopped as a few more clangs followed and then a flash of white followed by a blur of yellow ran past me and Magnus. I realized Storm had somehow managed to get loose from wherever Ronan had stashed her and was chasing Tink. Several guests tried to grab Storm as she flew past them, but she easily dodged them and headed right for Matty after Tink disappeared under a row of chairs. In her excitement, the puppy ran into Matty, knocking him to the ground.

"Matty," I called and started moving forward, but I'd only gotten a few steps when I saw Dante, who'd been sitting in a nearby guest chair, step into the aisle.

He grabbed the overly excited Storm and held her as he scooped Matty up and put him onto his feet. My son appeared unhurt, but I saw him patting his pocket and then his face fell as he began frantically looking around. It took me a moment to realize one or both rings had fallen out of his pocket.

I was about to go to him when I saw Dante gently take hold of Matty's arm and say something to him. I felt Magnus stiffen next to me. I grabbed him before he could stride forward and I didn't miss the fact that his hard eyes were on Dante as the young man spoke to Matty. All the other guests had quieted as the man and boy spoke and then Dante was pointing to the ground near one of the chairs. Matty quickly snatched up the ring and put it back in his pocket.

I couldn't hear what Dante was saying to him, but whatever it was, it had Matty smiling wide and then he patted Storm's head before he gave Dante a hug. Dante pointed to Seth and Ronan who'd each started back down the aisle before stopping when they'd seen Dante helping Matty. Matty continued walking as Tristan started playing again and I saw Dante lift the fifty pound plus puppy in his arms and carry her off to the side of the room where he set her down and held on to her. I glanced at Magnus so we could continue our walk side by side and saw that his eyes were still on Dante.

And Dante's were on his.

And for the first time since I'd known the young man, he actually looked embarrassed. It wasn't until he dropped his eyes that Magnus seemed to remember where we were and we continued making our way down the aisle. Once we reached the end, Magnus shook my hand and pulled me into an embrace. "Congratulations, Hawke," was all he said.

I nodded and stepped forward to where Ronan was standing, but I dropped down in front of Matty and said, "Are you okay, buddy?"

Matty nodded. "I've still got them, Papa," he said as he patted his pocket.

I laughed and kissed his cheek. I stood and locked eyes with Ronan briefly before I took my place by the minister. I sucked in a breath as I turned to watch for Tate. When I finally laid eyes on him, I had to lock my knees at the sight of him.

To say he looked gorgeous in his tux wasn't enough. But it wasn't even the way the fine material molded to his perfect body that had me struggling to draw in air. It was the light shining from his eyes that had my heart doing cartwheels. Pure joy radiated from him as he entered the room, his mother at his side and clinging to his arm. His eyes immediately sought out mine and I was sure I was going to pass out from the lack of oxygen. I actually swayed so badly that the minister said, "You okay, son?"

I was fucking perfect. I managed to filter myself as I said, "I'm good," but I didn't take my eyes off Tate as I spoke.

On the one hand, it seemed like it took forever for Tate to reach me, but on the other, I could have stood there all day just drinking in the sight of him. When he reached the platform, he gave his mom a kiss and wiped at her face, presumably to dash away the stray tear that had slid down her cheek. She said something to him and he nodded before releasing her so she could join her husband and daughters in the front row. When Tate turned back to me, I ignored protocol and stepped forward to take his hand. As soon as he had stepped up the two stairs and was level with me, I brushed my mouth over his.

"Hi," I said softly against his mouth.

"Hi," he responded and then he kissed me back. I heard the minister clearing his throat and I could honestly say that was the only thing that kept me from plunging my tongue into Tate's mouth the way I wanted.

"I got your message," Tate said as his thumb came up to brush my jaw line and I remembered the message I'd asked Matty to give to him. "I can't wait to marry you either," Tate whispered and then he kissed me again.

I smiled and tightened my hand on his before leading him to the minister. The man had a broad smile across his face so I knew our little deviation hadn't bothered him in the least. The man directed his attention to the crowd and said, "I usually use this time to share with everyone what I've learned about the couple who've honored me with helping them show their commitment to one another. But I don't think there are any words I could come up with that could better demonstrate the love we just saw that Michael and Tate have for each other. So I'd like to invite them to commit themselves to one another with the vows they've written."

I felt my heart lurch as Tate took my other hand in his and faced me.

"Tate, would you like to begin?" the minister asked and Tate nodded, his bright eyes never leaving mine.

"I never knew what lay on the other side of those storm clouds I dreamed of someday having the courage to fly into. And I didn't know how many there would be or how hard they would try to knock me from the sky. I thought…" Tate's voice caught and I felt tears sting my eyes as he fought to keep his own tears at bay. "I thought I'd have to weather those storms alone…that I'd have to be strong enough to fly through them to make it to the light on the other side." Tate shook his head. "But I don't have to be strong all the time. I can falter and there will be someone to catch me…to cast me back into the sky…to fly by my side when I don't think I can go on…when I can't fight another battle."

Tate's eyes shifted for a split second and I knew his eyes were on our son because the tears did begin to fall. He returned his gaze to me and said, "You told me once that I didn't have to pretend anymore. Do you remember that?"

I nodded because I remembered the moment perfectly. "I remember," I said hoarsely.

"Never again, Michael," he said. "Never again do I have to

dream of perfection, because it's right here." His finger began rubbing over my left ring finger…my too naked ring finger. "I love you, Michael. Forever and ever."

I laughed at that and I couldn't stop myself from lifting one of his hands to my lips to kiss it. Tate smiled and then he was trying to use his upper arms to dash at his tears so he wouldn't have to release my hands.

"Michael," the minister said softly.

I sucked in a breath. But the carefully crafted words I'd prepared wouldn't come. I'd pored through various Internet sites to find the perfect combination of words to say to this man who'd changed my life…saved it, but even now they didn't ring true. The realization that I was suddenly without vows should have scared me, but it didn't. Because being in front of Tate, holding him, seeing how much he really loved me, made the words flow without any effort at all.

"I died ten years ago. Pure and simple," I whispered. "I went on breathing, walking, talking…but that was it. There was no such thing as joy or hope. There was no need for a future…no desire for one, either."

I saw Tate nod in understanding and he didn't even try to stop the tears that fell. Only he could understand the agony I'd felt because he'd been the only one brave enough to see the real me… he'd been the only one strong enough to love the real me.

"And then I crashed through a door and into a life I didn't even know was possible."

Tate smiled at the subtle reference I'd made to the day we'd met.

"I hated you," I admitted as my throat threatened to close up. Tate nodded and I knew he understood what I meant.

"I hated that you made me feel again…I hated that you made me want things I'd accepted I would never have. I hated that I loved you so damn much. I hated that I ever let you think I didn't. I hated that I let you walk away. I hated that I didn't chase you down and hold on to you so damn tight that you'd never be able to make a move again without me by your side. I hated that I ever made you doubt yourself and how beautiful and strong and amazing you are."

I blinked the tears that were blurring my vision away, not caring who saw them fall.

"There are moments where I can't breathe when I'm around you," I admitted. "And sometimes I can't breathe when you're not around," I said with a chuckle. Tate let out a soft laugh and nodded in agreement. "I love you, Tate. For all the things you've given me and for all the things you've taken away. For making every breath that I do take worth taking. For showing me I don't have to forget the past to have a future with you and our son. For making me realize what 'forever and ever' really means and for letting me love you that way. I love you," I whispered and then I leaned in to kiss him.

"I love you," Tate breathed against my mouth.

"Okay, I'm thinking we need to do the short, short version," the minister said with a chuckle. Tate and I both laughed and forced some space between our bodies.

"Can we have the rings please?" the man asked.

Matty walked up the steps and stood in front of us, a big grin on his face. Tate and I both reached down to pat him on the back. Matty pulled the rings out and held his palm out.

"Tate, please place your ring on Michael's finger and repeat after me."

The metal of the platinum ring felt amazing against my skin as Tate slid it onto my finger and I barely heard the words he repeated. When it was my turn, I had to focus on every word the minister was saying or there was no way I was going to get through them. Tate let out a small gasp when I slid the ring on his finger and he closed his eyes as more tears fell.

By the time the minister announced us as wed, I was already pulling Tate into my arms and sealing my mouth over his. I tuned out everyone else but him and me and told him with my touch the things I hadn't been able to convey with mere words.

I was dimly aware of applause and Ronan and Seth offering their congratulations to each of us. I reached down to pick up Matty and then the three of us were holding onto each other as we pledged our love to one another forever and ever. By the time we were ready to walk down the aisle, I was glad to see that we weren't the only ones in tears.

But nothing sounded better then when the minister announced us as Michael, Tate and Matthew Hawkins.

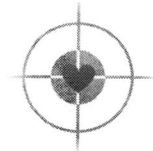

Chapter 16

MAV

"Merry Christmas, Mav," Eli whispered against my mouth.

"It's not Christmas yet," I murmured as I drew him closer to me, though there was no room left between us.

"Yes it is," he said. "It's 12:01."

I chuckled as I realized we'd been slow dancing for a couple of hours. After we'd said our goodbyes to Hawke and Tate who'd wanted to get Matty home to bed, as well as to Ronan, Seth and their new posse of little ones, Eli had dragged me on the dance floor insisting that we dance…another first for me and one I was glad for because any excuse to have his body pressed flush against mine was fine by me. Even when the DJ had played more upbeat music, we'd stayed in our quiet corner and swayed back and forth, oblivious to the couples around us who'd joined us on the dance floor.

I knew we'd need to get on the road within a couple of hours so that we could be home to spend Christmas morning with Caleb, Eli's mother and Jace, but I figured reality could wait a bit longer. And reality was going better than I could have hoped for. When Eli had spoken to Caleb earlier in the evening, he'd put the phone on speaker and I'd heard for myself how relaxed and happy Caleb had actually sounded as he'd told us what he and Jace had done during the day and how they had plans to go to Mariana's house for dinner.

But as pleased as I'd been to know that Caleb had had a good day, I knew another fall was coming when Jace had to leave. Even if the man lived in the area, it was a relationship that neither he nor I could in good faith encourage. Caleb was clearly more than just "attached" to the man and while I couldn't necessarily fault the age gap between them since there was a similar age spread between me and Eli, I knew Caleb was so messed up in the head that he wasn't in any position to think rationally about a physical or emotional relationship with an older man who wasn't looking for commitment.

"Mav."

I reluctantly released my grip on Eli so I could turn around to see who'd called my name and I saw Mace approaching me. Cole and Jonas stood just a few feet away, arms around one another and their luggage in hand. "You heading out?" I asked as I leaned in to hug Mace.

The man nodded. "We need to be in the Hamptons first thing."

I knew Mace and his men were spending Christmas with Jonas's best friend Casey, her husband and their three children. "Glad you guys were able to make it," I said as I slapped him on the back.

"Us too," Mace responded and then he was hugging Eli. "Eli, good to see you again and glad to hear you've agreed to make an honest man out of this one," he said with a chuckle.

Eli laughed and then he was pressing against my side. "Have a safe trip home."

"Will do," Mace said and then he was patting me on the arm before turning away. I saw him take Jonas's outstretched hand and then they left the house.

A glance around the dance floor showed that the party was winding down and there were only a handful of couples remaining. "We definitely need to have this at our wedding," I murmured as I motioned to the dance floor before drawing Eli back into my arms.

"Definitely," Eli agreed. "But let's skip the dog chasing the cat down the aisle."

I laughed. "Baby's too damn lazy to chase anything."

Eli gave me a light punch on the chest and then he was dragging me down for a lusty kiss. "I can't wait to marry you," he said against my mouth.

"Vegas is a short flight away," I offered as I tried to catch my breath. "I can probably commandeer Ronan and Seth's jet."

Eli smiled and said. "Sure, and then you can explain to my mother *and* Dom and Logan that we got married without them."

I nodded. "Point taken."

"It's going to be perfect, Mav," Eli said softly as he played with the engagement ring he'd finally put on my finger a few nights earlier.

I tipped his chin up and said, "It already is, Eli."

And then I kissed him before I got us moving again.

Because reality *could* wait a couple more hours. And when we were finally forced to meet it head on, we'd do it…together.

Chapter 17

RONAN

WHILE MY INTENT HAD BEEN TO WAKE MY HUSBAND UP EARLY ON Christmas morning with some soft, gentle kisses that would hopefully lead to more than just kissing, my plan was thwarted by a small body that surprisingly took up a lot of space. Not to mention the Spiderman doll that was nudged up under my armpit.

I hadn't even heard Jamie sneak into bed with us during the night, but I definitely didn't have a problem with it. Especially not with how cute he looked all snuggled up against Seth's chest and Seth holding him protectively with one arm. I supposed it was a habit we shouldn't be encouraging, but for now it wasn't something I would have changed for anything. A glance at the clock showed it was pretty late considering it was Christmas morning, but it wasn't really all that surprising considering it had been well after midnight by the time we'd gotten home. The kids had been tired, but they'd seemed to have had a good time at the wedding. At one point Seth had even managed to get little Nicole out on the dance floor when they'd been doing one of the dances that appeared to have a choreographed routine associated with it. Nicole hadn't heard the music, of course, but I suspected she'd felt the vibrations. She'd been nervous at first, but as soon as Jamie, Matty and Leo had joined

Seth and started following along with the routine, Nicole had gotten in on the act and she'd been all smiles by the time the song had ended and she'd gone back to the safety of her sister's company.

Willow hadn't been able to do much since she was limited as to how much she could move around, but Hannah had spent most of the reception by her side and I'd often seen the girls talking and laughing as they'd discussed whatever it was that teenage girls talked about.

I forced myself out of bed and went to the bathroom to take care of business before searching out my pajama top. Bullet eyed me from where he'd stolen my spot on the bed and he actually dropped his big head to my pillow when I shook my head at him. I chuckled and then went around the bed to drop a soft kiss on Seth's temple before leaving the room. I could already smell the coffee brewing as I neared the kitchen, but I was surprised to find the room wasn't empty. Nicole was sitting in one of the kitchen chairs facing the window, her eyes on the light snow falling outside. Since I didn't want to startle her, I flipped the light switch for the chandelier above the table a few times. She turned slowly in her chair to look at me, but didn't react in any other way. I went to the table and sat next to her, concerned by her solemn expression.

Seth and I had had multiple sessions with a sign language teacher, but we were far from fluent. I mentally crossed my fingers and signed what I hoped were the right words.

Everything okay?

Nicole nodded, but didn't sign anything back.

Did you sleep okay?

That question earned me another nod, but nothing more.

Are you hungry?

This time a shake of the head.

I tapped my fingers on the table as I thought about what to say next, but Nicole beat me to the punch and began signing. Relief went through me when I recognized the words.

Merry Christmas.

I smiled and signed the words back to her and added her name for good measure. She smiled and then she was sliding a piece of paper that had been sitting face down on the table in front of her across to me.

I turned it over and felt my insides light up at the sight of five carefully drawn people and a dog in front of a house that had the same colors as our house. One of the taller people had dark hair, the other one had blond hair.

Is this for me? I signed.

Nicole nodded and then pointed to the blond-haired figure.

And Seth?

Another nod.

I felt tears threatening, but I managed to hold them back.

Thank you.

You're welcome.

I carefully reached out to touch her cheek and she let me. I took the picture over to the refrigerator and stuck it on it with a couple of magnets. I searched the cabinet for the package of instant hot chocolate Seth and I had bought in anticipation of the kids' arrival and took it along with a bag of marshmallows back to Nicole and showed it to her. She nodded without me even needing to ask her if she wanted them. I got her drink ready and tossed a few marshmallows in and then took the rest of the bag back to the table along with the mug. As she topped off the drink with an insane number of marshmallows, I got myself a cup of coffee.

We sat in silence for a few minutes just drinking and watching the snow fall, but when I saw Willow appear in the doorway to the kitchen, I got Nicole's attention and pointed behind her. Nicole got out of her chair and ran to her sister and hugged her. They began signing back and forth, but their motions were too quick for me to catch much. The only words I got were *Merry Christmas*.

"Morning," I said to Willow as she stepped farther into the kitchen.

"Morning," she said quietly.

"How are you feeling?"

"Good," she responded. She was still clearly nervous around me, but I hadn't really expected anything different.

"Would you like some hot chocolate?"

Willow nodded and stood behind Nicole's chair as I prepared it. She ran her fingers over her sister's hair as Nicole drank. By the time I was putting her mug on the table, I heard the clicking of nails on hardwood and Bullet came trotting into the kitchen with Jamie right on his heels.

"Santa came!" he shouted and then he was throwing his arms around his sister's legs.

"How do you know?" Willow asked as she reached down to pick him up, but he squirmed out of her reach and grabbed her hand instead.

"Come on!" he ordered impatiently and then he was grabbing Nicole's hand. He practically dragged his sisters out of the kitchen and I saw Seth barely move out of their way in time as he reached the kitchen entry way.

His eyes fell on me and his already wide smile grew wider.

"Morning," I said softly and then he was walking into my arms.

"Morning," he murmured tiredly and then he was lifting his mouth to mine. The kiss was short and sweet…and utterly perfect. "Merry Christmas, Ronan."

"Merry Christmas, baby," I breathed against his lips before brushing another kiss over them. "Coffee?" I asked, but Seth didn't even get a chance to answer because Jamie rushed back into the room and grabbed both our hands and tried to pull us forward.

"Hurry up! He came!"

Seth and I both laughed and then Seth was letting himself be dragged out of the room. I snagged my coffee as I followed them to the living room. I leaned against the archway as I watched Jamie excitedly showing Seth all the presents beneath the tree. Nicole was standing shyly next to them and I saw Seth signing *Merry Christmas* to her. She smiled and then hugged him before dropping to her knees to start rifling through the presents and sorting them.

"Um, Dr. Grisham?"

Willow approached me slowly from where she'd been standing off to the side watching her brother and sister.

"You can call me Ronan," I reminded her. I hated that she felt the need for such formality with us, but I knew it would likely be a while before she became comfortable enough to really see us as anything besides a temporary way station in the chaotic journey she and her siblings had been on in the past year.

"Ronan," she said, as if testing the sound of my name. "I was wondering...we were wondering," she said as she motioned to her brother and sister. "If we could take you up on the offer to use the other bedrooms?"

I hid the joy that rushed through me at the question. I knew that Willow had insisted the trio share one room as a way of keeping her brother and sister close, so to have her be the one to ask if they could each have their own room was a huge step forward. I managed to play it cool as I said, "Of course. We can move you into them today if you want."

Willow nodded. She shifted back and forth on her feet, but remained quiet so I said, "Was there something else?"

"Um...Hannah was telling me that she and her friends are going to a movie tomorrow and she invited me to go. They're going for ice cream afterwards, but the ice cream store is just a couple doors down from the theater so I wouldn't have to walk much...so I was just wondering if I could go."

"Of course you can," I said, again hiding the fact that I was practically doing cartwheels on the inside. "I'll talk to her fathers today at Christmas dinner to make the arrangements."

Willow nodded and a small smile graced her lips. "Thank you."

I wanted so badly to reach out and touch her, but I didn't.

"You're welcome."

I thought for sure that was it. That she'd turn away and go to her brother and sister and start looking through all the presents, but she surprised me yet again when she slowly approached me and then pushed into my arms. I automatically wrapped my free arm around her since my other one still had the cup of coffee in it.

"Merry Christmas, Ronan."

My voice was so thick with emotion that I barely managed to get out, "Merry Christmas, Willow." I dropped a kiss to the top of her head and then saw Seth watching us both with a big smile on his face. Willow glanced up at me shyly as she released me and then she was heading towards Jamie and Nicole. Seth passed her as he was walking towards me and she graced him with the same hug she'd given me.

I put my arm out long before Seth reached me and he automatically walked into my embrace and leaned against my side. He didn't say anything and neither did I. We didn't need to. He merely brushed his mouth over mine in the sweetest of kisses and then we both turned to revel in the sight of our new family enjoying the first of what I knew would be many Christmases to come.

Epilogue

MAGNUS

"Someone's here, Pop-pop," Matty said at the sound of the doorbell ringing. He wriggled out of the shirt I'd just started trying to get over his head and began running towards the front door.

"Matty, don't open it," I called as I climbed to my feet and hurried after him, his shirt still in my hand. It was only eight o' clock at night, but since it was pitch dark outside, I wasn't about to let him answer the door on his own.

"It's Dante," Matty said as he peeked through the long window next to the door. My stomach automatically did the uncomfortable flip it always did when I heard the man's name, but I ignored it and steeled myself as I reached for the doorknob. I was still pissed about the sight I'd walked in on in the guest bathroom after the wedding ceremony the day before.

I ignored the voice that reminded me that pissed wasn't all I'd felt at the sight of Dante with his dick shoved down some guy's throat.

Dante was leaning negligently against the doorframe, his mouth pulled into a slight smirk as his eyes settled on me. "Hey, Pop-pop," he said.

Irritation went through me, but I ignored it and reacted exactly the way I knew Dante would hate.

By not reacting at all.

Dante's eyes narrowed just slightly at my lack of comment and I saw the grin on his mouth thin just a little.

"Dante," Matty said excitedly and Dante ripped his eyes from me and dropped to his knees and embraced the little boy, mindful of the central line on Matty's chest. While Matty and the rest of us had gotten used to the two cannulas that protruded from his small body, I couldn't wait for the damn things to be removed. It would be proof that my grandson was well on his way to a complete recovery and I wouldn't have to face the fear of losing him on a daily basis. But for now, he still needed regular rounds of medications and the central line was the most effective way to administer them.

"I brought you something," Dante said and he produced a package wrapped in newspaper. "Merry Christmas, Matty," he offered as he handed the present over.

Matty's eyes went wide and he quickly looked up at me. "Can I open it, Pop-pop?"

I nodded and then held the door open wider for Dante when he looked at me questioningly. I may not like the man much, but he'd been kind to Matty in the months he'd been protecting him. My thoughts drifted to the day before when Storm had accidentally knocked Matty down during the wedding ceremony. I hadn't known what to expect when Dante had helped Matty to his feet and then whispered something to him that'd had the crestfallen boy doing a one-eighty and smiling happily despite the upsetting event.

Dante followed Matty into the living room and sat down next to him on the couch to help him unwrap the present where there was just a little too much tape. Matty's eyes went wide when he saw the doll. "It's Magneto!" he cried out excitedly.

"I heard you really wanted him to add to your collection," Dante said.

Matty nodded. "Thank you!" he said as he threw his arms around Dante before ripping into the plastic to try and work the doll free. Dante took it from him and began opening it so Matty wouldn't hurt himself on the tough plastic.

"Why'd you want him?" Dante asked as he worked. "Isn't Magneto the bad guy?"

"Nah," Matty said as he tugged at some loose tape on the box. "He's really a good guy, but sometimes he just does bad things."

I watched in surprise as Dante paused in what he was doing. It took him several long seconds to focus again and when he shot me a quick glance, I didn't see any of the usual cocky arrogance I'd come to accept as part of the man's genetic makeup.

Dante increased his efforts to get the doll loose from its housing and then he was handing it to Matty.

"Thank you," Matty said happily and he gave Dante another hug.

"You're welcome," Dante whispered and I saw him drop his mouth to the top of Matty's head like he was going to kiss him. A look of pain shimmered in his gaze just before he closed his eyes and just held on to Matty for a moment.

The whole thing lasted no more than ten seconds, but it left me feeling shaky, though I wasn't sure why. Dante pulled back from Matty and studied him for a moment before his eyes shifted to me. I saw the moment a curtain fell into place and Dante's solemn expression morphed into the 'I don't give a shit about anything' one that I hated.

"Have a good time at Disney World," Dante offered to Matty as he stood. Matty merely nodded, too enraptured with his new toy to do much else.

"See you soon, Pop-pop," Dante said to me in a low drawl before turning and walking out of the house. I cursed myself for allowing the man to have me second guessing myself for even a moment.

Dante Thorne was an asshole, through and through.

And I was stuck with him for the next few weeks or for however long it took to close one last chapter in my life before embarking on a new journey.

"Okay, Matty, bed time," I said as I sat down next to him and put his pajama top on him. He took my hand in his and led me to his bedroom. I'd already pulled his covers aside so he climbed into bed, the Magneto doll still in his hand.

Once I had him settled under the covers, I reached for the two books he'd selected for me to read to him.

"Pop-pop, can I tell you a secret?"

"Of course you can," I responded as I put the books on the bed and gave him my full attention. He'd finally started to put on some weight in the month that he'd been out of the hospital and I could see the slightest shadow of hair growth on his head.

"I'm going to marry Leo someday."

I smiled at that. "You are?" I asked.

Matty nodded.

"Does he want to marry you?"

Another nod and then Matty was sitting up. "We talked about it. He's my best friend like Daddy is Papa's best friend. And I'm his."

"Okay, is that the only reason?"

Matty shook his head. "He doesn't like broccoli and I don't like peas." Before I could even try to decode the odd statement, Matty said, "He'll eat my peas and I'll eat his broccoli."

"Ah, I see," I said. "What else?"

"We both think our daddies kiss too much so we're not gonna."

I chuckled. "Those sound like really good reasons to get married," I responded. "But maybe wait a few years just to be sure."

"Pop-pop, are you gonna get married?"

"Maybe," I hedged. No reason to tell him there was no chance in hell that would ever happen. I'd been there and I'd definitely done that.

Never again.

"You could marry Dante."

I stilled at that, unsure of what to say. "Why do you think me and Dante should get married?" I asked. I wasn't particularly keen on explaining to Matty the facts of life, including that unlike most of the men in his life, his grandfather wasn't interested in members of his own sex.

A flash of heat went through me when I remembered the sight

of Dante's hand resting on the head of the guy who'd been blowing him.

Fuck.

"Because Dante is alone and you're alone," Matty stated as he toyed with his doll. "If you get married, you won't be alone anymore. Like Papa and Daddy were alone before they met."

"Your daddy had you," I reminded him, more to get him off the topic of me and the dark-eyed man who even now was burrowed a little too far under my skin for my liking.

"But he was still sad all the time," Matty said softly and then he was sitting up. He dropped his doll into his lap and then put his tiny hands on my cheeks. "Like you, Pop-pop."

I felt my chest tighten. My grandson was just too damn perceptive.

"I'll think about it," I said, now very eager to end the discussion.

Matty held onto me for a moment and then he was wrapping his arms around my neck. "I'm going to miss you, Pop-pop," he whispered.

I held his body against mine and swallowed down the emotion that suddenly was making it hard to talk. "I'm gonna miss you too, buddy."

"You're gonna come back, right?"

I nodded against him. Early on when I'd first met Hawke and Tate and had been reunited with the little boy I'd thought had been lost to me forever, I hadn't been certain that I'd want to give up my life in Texas, but it had taken just a few days in Matty's presence to know that my life was with him, no matter what I was giving up to make that happen.

"I'm coming back," I assured him and then I was getting him settled back under the covers. I grabbed one of the books before Matty could start spouting off the benefits of a relationship between me and his very irritating bodyguard and flipped it open.

"Pop-pop," Matty whispered.

"Yeah," I said.

"Will you tell me about my Mama?"

I sucked in a breath at that because it was the first time Matty had even mentioned his mother. Pain radiated out through all my limbs and for a second I actually wondered if I was having a heart attack. I managed to compose myself and wiped at the tears I could feel gathering at the corners of my eyes.

"When I come back, I'll tell you all about her. Deal?" I asked.

Matty nodded. He was quiet for a moment before saying, "Did she love me, Pop-pop?"

"She did, buddy," I said.

"As much as you do?"

I bit into my lip hard and nodded. "Yep, just as much as I do."

Matty smiled. "That's a lot."

I laughed and wiped at my eyes again. "Yeah it is."

We both fell silent, but I didn't realize I'd gotten lost in my thoughts until Matty gently touched the book I was holding open in my hands. "Read the story, Pop-pop."

I nodded and began reading.

Anything to keep my mind off the daughter who would never get to see her son grow up.

And the man who knew how to push all my buttons and then some.

The End

Scroll to the next page to check out a bonus scene

Bonus Scene

DOM

DECEMBER 25ᵀᴴ

"Merry Christmas, Dom."

I smiled at the feel of Logan's fingers skimming over my head. Even after nine years together, he was still just as fascinated with my bald head as he'd ever been.

"Merry Christmas, Logan," I said softly.

I was lying where I often ended up – with my head on his bare chest, my arm wrapped around his waist. It was the same position I'd been in nine years earlier when I'd woken up to find that I hadn't dreamed the night before when he'd come to me and changed our trajectory forever.

I still remembered everything about that night and the hours that had followed. I'd been mourning not just the loss of Sylvie, but the loss of Logan as well. There'd been no family to lean on so I'd retreated to my island house in the desperate hope of finding some kind of solace in the place that Sylvie and I had spent so many Christmases together…and the first place I'd been with Logan and accepted that my life hadn't ended just because I'd lost my wife.

I'd kept myself busy by starting the process of putting Sylvie's things away so that I'd be ready to donate the things I had no use for and stashing away the things I'd wanted to keep that I would someday be strong enough to bring out into the open and use to remember everything about the woman who'd been my entire world. But there'd been no amount of distraction that had eased the pain of losing Logan…of remembering the final words I'd said to him…the words he'd accepted.

I have to stay away from you.

They'd been the hardest words I'd ever had to say. Walking away from him that day had been just as hard. I'd died all over again just like I had when I'd watched Sylvie's gaunt but still beautiful face being covered up with a sheet after she'd taken her last breath.

And then I'd turned around and he'd been there.

Logan was fond of telling people that I'd given him a second chance, but I'd never seen it that way. I'd been the one with the second chance, though I nearly hadn't taken it. He'd turned his back on me after I'd told him it was too late…that he was too late. And I'd died another death all over again.

But then God or Sylvie or whatever force had driven us together in the first place had taken one last chance on us and I'd grabbed his arm and dragged him back to me.

And I hadn't ever let him go again.

Nine years later and everything had changed and yet in so many ways they hadn't. Yes, we were older, a little heavier, our bodies weren't as perfect as they'd once been, but I still felt my breath catch every time I looked at Logan. I still felt that moment of pure rightness go through me when his pale blue eyes settled on me.

Nine years and four kids later and we were still the same two men we'd been that night. I ached for him now like I had then.

I turned so I was facing him and smiled when his hand came down to cup my chin. I lifted enough to meet the kiss he gave me.

For the past eight years, Logan had woken me up just after midnight on Christmas day to wish me a Merry Christmas. We'd ended up adopting Tristan shortly after we'd gotten married so our first Christmas after the one that had brought us back together hadn't allowed for us to do what we'd done that first morning… spending the day making love. So, we'd had to adjust a bit to accommodate a busy schedule of putting presents under the tree and waiting for our kids to rouse us from our pretend sleep to proclaim that Santa had come. But for a few hours just after the stroke of midnight, we belonged just to each other again like we had that night.

"The wedding was beautiful, wasn't it?" Logan murmured as his hand skimmed down my side. I felt my already hard cock growing stiffer with his touch.

"Mmmmm," I managed to get out as I put my hand on top of Logan's in the hopes of guiding it to where I needed it most.

He chuckled and captured my fingers with his and then linked our hands together before unlinking them.

"And Eli...did you see how happy he was?" Logan asked, his voice growing thick.

I felt tears pricking my own eyes as I thought about the joy I'd seen on my oldest child's face when he'd shown us the ring Mav had given him. I'd made a terrible mistake in not showing and telling Eli early on in our relationship that mine and Logan's love for him equaled that of parents loving a child. I knew he knew it now, but it had come at a high price and it was something I would struggle with for the rest of my life. The consolation was that I'd never seen Eli happier than he was with Mav.

"We went too easy on Mav," I said with a smile as I remembered the man's nervousness as he'd sat in our kitchen a few weeks earlier trying to gather the courage to ask our permission to marry our son.

"We'll make Memphis squirm a bit before we say yes," Logan suggested and I laughed. Seeing both my sons in happy relationships was an amazing thing, but I was also very glad that it would be a long while before Tanner was old enough to find his other half.

And Sylvie...hell, if I had my way, Sylvie would stay a little girl forever.

But of course since she was four going on forty, I knew we weren't going to be that lucky. I could only hope that whatever life partner or partners she chose would have even half the strength and integrity of the men our sons had chosen.

"I dreamed of this," Logan said softly as he continued to play with my fingers. I looked up at him and saw his beautiful eyes full of such emotion that I had to sit up and put my hand against his cheek.

"You dreamed of what, baby?" I asked as I caressed his skin with my thumb.

"That night that I came back to you. After we made love, I was watching you sleep and I dreamed that we'd have this. Kids, family...this," he whispered as he motioned between us.

I leaned in to kiss him. "I didn't need to dream it," I told him. "I knew the second you walked through that door that you were mine and that we would have this. My brain was still trying to protect my heart, but my heart had already decided."

Tears slipped down Logan's face. "I was so scared you weren't going to stop me that night," he managed to get out.

"Letting you go was never an option," I said softly before I kissed him. He automatically opened his mouth for me and then his arms were wrapping around my back. I pulled back and cupped his face. "When I do let you go, it will only be because there's no life left in my fingers to hold on to you, do you hear me?"

Logan nodded. He brushed a kiss over my lips and then said, "When that day comes, I'm not letting you go. Wherever you go, I go. In this life or the next."

My body shook with the sudden need that rushed over me. "I love you," I ground out before I took over his mouth. I heard the words whispered back to me between kisses, but I was too far gone to do anything but drink them down. I maneuvered us until Logan was lying beneath me. I felt his hands slip beneath my pajama bottoms to grip my ass as I kissed him and ground my cock against his. I lifted off Logan long enough to strip his pants and mine off and grab the lube from the nightstand drawer. He was waiting for me with open arms when I dropped my weight back down on him and I felt his legs wrap around my waist.

"I can't wait," I said hoarsely as I reached between our bodies and lubed up my cock. I added some to Logan's as well and began stroking his shaft with my slick hand as my dick sought out his hole.

I used my arms to move Logan's legs so they were wide and high, splitting him open for my seeking dick. I'd been extra generous with the lube so I made sure to rub my crown and shaft over his hole to add a layer of the slick substance before I sought out his mouth with mine and shifted into position.

Logan cried out as my dick began opening him up. I eagerly drank down the sound along with every grunt and moan he gave me as I slid deeper into his hot, willing body. I felt his fingers gripping my head and the sensation just caused more excitement to flood my nerve endings. I drove into my husband with one hard push until my balls brushed up against his ass.

"Yes, Dom!" Logan cried out as his hands moved to my back and scraped across my skin.

Even all these years later and still my man's body was so fucking tight that it felt like he'd been made just for me…a perfect fit.

I pulled out and slid in again as I used my tongue to lick at the sweat that had started collecting on Logan's neck.

"Fuck, more," Logan demanded as he lowered his legs and grabbed my ass with his hands.

"So perfect," I murmured as I nipped at Logan's lips. I pulled my dick out of him almost all the way before shoving back in to the root.

"Yes!" Logan hissed as his fingers bit into my ass trying to draw me deeper inside of him.

"Do you need more, baby?" I asked as I continued with slow, smooth glides.

Logan eagerly nodded.

I used my hands to lift his legs and fold them in on himself, lifting his ass higher off the bed. I changed the angle of my hips and drove into him hard and fast, nailing his prostate as I went.

"Fuck, yes! Dom!"

I put his legs over my shoulders and then dropped my weight down on him so I could kiss him. Since I didn't want him to have to hold the position too long, I began fucking him hard, making sure my dick hit his gland with every pass. I captured the wail of pleasure that escaped Logan's throat and kept up the brutal pace until I felt his inner muscles start to clamp down on me with impossible pressure. I slid a hand between our bodies and felt his dick pulsing wildly. It would take very little to drive him over the edge.

"Logan, look at me," I ordered.

Logan opened his eyes and he held my gaze as I slowly lowered his legs so he could wrap them around my waist. "I never would have let you go," I whispered. I knew they were words he needed to hear because I knew he hung on to the darker moments of our past, wondering if he could have spared us both from the cruel wounds we'd inflicted upon one another as we'd tried to find our way. Logan was just that type of person…he held things closer, deeper, and longer than most. And I didn't want him to spend even one second wondering what our lives would have been like if he'd walked out that door…if I hadn't stopped him.

Logan nodded. "I love you so much, Dom. As much now as then. Not more because that just isn't possible."

I smiled and I kissed him softly. "I love you, Logan. Then, now, forever. Doesn't matter. I will always love you."

I began moving again, but there was no longer any room for the frantic pace we'd been setting. Instead, we moved as one because that was what we'd become the moment he'd chosen to honor the wishes of the woman I'd loved and lost…the woman who'd loved me as much as Logan did and had given me the future she and I hadn't been meant to have.

The orgasm was violent, but in a quiet way. We clung to each other as the pleasure rippled through us in nearly simultaneous waves. If I hadn't known any better, I would have sworn it was one orgasm tumbling through us. I buried my face in Logan's neck as I succumbed to the pleasure and purpose this man gave me on every level. I could have been there for minutes or hours, my body still buried deep inside of his, when I felt his lips brushing my temple.

"Come shower with me," Logan murmured and I lifted my head long enough to kiss him and nod.

Because I knew what would happen next and I welcomed it. We'd end up showering together which would ultimately lead to another round of lovemaking. But after that as I began the process of putting the countless presents under the giant Christmas tree in our living room, I'd lose my husband to what I knew was a bittersweet tradition for him.

Because as with all the previous Christmases, Logan had a letter to write and I knew he would struggle with it. After all, how did you thank someone for selflessly giving you the life they should have had?

But I knew my Logan would find a way…he always did.

Also by Sloane Kennedy

(Note: Not all titles will be available on all retail sites)

The Escort Series
Gabriel's Rule (M/F)

Shane's Fall (M/F)

Logan's Need (M/M)

Barretti Security Series
Loving Vin (M/F)

Redeeming Rafe (M/M)

Saving Ren (M/M/M)

Freeing Zane (M/M)

Finding Series
Finding Home (M/M/M)

Finding Trust (M/M)

Finding Peace (M/M)

Finding Forgiveness (M/M)

Finding Hope (M/M/M)

Love in Eden
Always Mine (M/M)

Pelican Bay Series
Locked in Silence (M/M)

Sanctuary Found (M/M)

The Truth Within (M/M)

The Protectors

Absolution (M/M/M)

Salvation (M/M)

Retribution (M/M)

Forsaken (M/M)

Vengeance (M/M/M)

A Protectors Family Christmas

Atonement (M/M)

Revelation (M/M)

Redemption (M/M)

Defiance (M/M)

Unexpected (M/M/M)

Shattered (M/M)

Unbroken (M/M)

Protecting Elliot: A Protectors Novella (M/M)

Discovering Daisy: A Protectors Novella (M/M/F)

Pretend You're Mine: A Protectors Short Story (M/M)

Non-Series

Four Ever (M/M/M/M)

Letting Go (M/F)

Short Stories

A Touch of Color

Catching Orion

Twist of Fate Series (co-writing with Lucy Lennox)

Lost and Found (M/M)

Safe and Sound (M/M)

Body and Soul (M/M)

Crossover Books with Lucy Lennox

Made Mine: A Protectors/Made Marian Crossover (M/M)

The following titles are available in audiobook format with more on the way:

Locked in Silence

Sanctuary Found

The Truth Within

Absolution

Salvation

Retribution

Logan's Need

Redeeming Rafe

Saving Ren

Freeing Zane

Forsaken

Vengeance

Finding Home

Finding Trust

Finding Peace

Four Ever

Lost and Found

Safe and Sound

Body and Soul

Made Mine

Printed in Great Britain
by Amazon